To:

Efo Atsu

Warm Regards

Senna

July 2020.

An Inconvenient Shadow

By

Senna Tagboto

Apart from the true story of my ancestor being thrown overboard, the characters depicted in this novel are fictitious. Any similarity to any person living or dead is merely coincidental.

An Inconvenient Shadow
Copyright © 2018 Senna Tagboto
All rights reserved

The Publishers,
An Inconvenient Shadow,
7795 Glade Bend,
Fairburn, GA 30213
Contact: aninconvenientshadow2018@gmail.com

ISBN-13: 978-1-7328904-1-1 (Paperback)

ISBN 978-1-7328904-0-4 (ebook)

Cover design by G A Creative Consult, Canada.

Authors photograph © CustoMYzeMe, Dallas, Texas.

Cover background photograph: "Sunset at Kete-Krachi" by Yaw Pare, Ghana.

First Edition Printing November 2018

Printed and bound in the United States of America

This novel is dedicated to those who have gone before us, who left numerous stories behind...

To my father, Dr. Emmanuel Kofi Tagboto, who fascinated us with his endless repertoire of stories. My aunt, Esther Kwawukume who kept all the oral traditions of our family intact, and my ancestor, Elias Mensah "Nukpese" Quist, who inspired this story.

Acknowledgements

I would like to thank my Editor, Michele Ben, for her invaluable critique and for not letting me get away with anything less than my best.

Thank you, Stanley Abotsi, for your input, your encouragement and for translating the needed text into West Indian Creole.

To Doran Parker-Knapp, Bella Ayivie Tamaklo, Wanda Cahoon and Sheila Akyea for reading everything and for your honest feedback. Your critique was invaluable!

My sincere appreciation goes to Mr. William Sohne, who researched and published the Quist family's genealogical register.

Special thanks to Teddy Osei of *Osibisa*, who gave me permission to use their song "Welcome Home" in the novel.

I appreciate Mr. C.K. Ladzekpo for translating and giving me the history behind the Ewe songs.

Also, to the Staff of Parr Library, Plano Texas who searched high and low and found me anything I needed to research this book, thank you.

My eternal thanks to The Almighty, the giver of the gift. How can I keep from singing your praise?

Note from the Author

The fascinating story of my ancestor, Elias Mensah Quist, (see family tree on the next page) who was thrown overboard, while on his way to visit his Danish father in Denmark in the 19th century, was well known among the descendants of the Quist family of Keta, Ghana.

For more than three decades, it was a story I knew my ancestors wanted me to write.

The books, Daughters of the Trade, by Pernille Ipsen (Associate Professor of Gender and Women's Studies and History) and Closing the Books, by the last Governor of the Guinea Coast, Edward Carstensen, gave color to the lives and the relationships between the Danish traders and the indigenes of the Guinea Coast, now Ghana.

Inspired by true events, this fictional novel gives a voice to the voiceless men and women of the 19th century.

Authors Family Tree

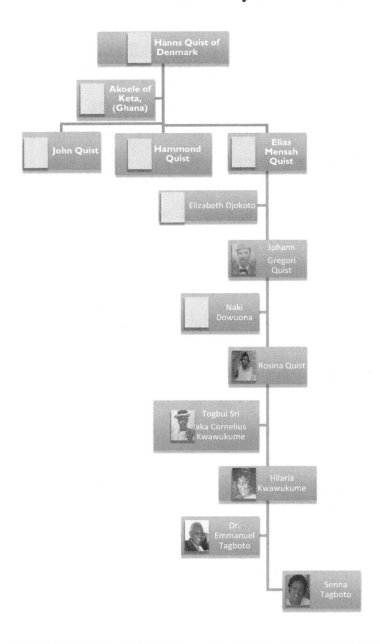

Table of Contents

An Inconvenient Shadow

Part one

"There are years that ask questions,

and

years that answer questions."

Zora Neale Hurston

1

Quitta,[1] March 1ˢᵗ, 1850

Kø sat in the sand, and out of habit, he dug his toes deep into the succulent, golden sand. He watched as the sand dribbled down, and sighed with pleasure as he enjoyed the soft warmth. He wiggled his toes a bit more till all that was left were brilliant flecks of gold, which stubbornly stuck to his feet. Then he set the miniature ship he had fashioned out with bits of rich, hard, dark *Odum* wood in the sand beside him. He stared out at sea towards the huge ship berthed about a mile away, squinting to blot out the dying sun's desperate orange rays. He could barely make out the name, *The Pharaoh*, written on the stern. He studied the ship's curves and angles with the practiced eye of a master carpenter. Slowly, he lifted his miniature to eye level as he compared the reality with the miniature. He let out a satisfied

[1] Keta is the capital of the **Keta Municipal District** of the Volta Region of Ghana. The Danes probably for phonetic reasons, spelled it - Quitta.

chuckle when he saw that what he had so painstakingly crafted was an exact copy.

He stared at the tiny portholes, the high masts and the ornate carving of an angel blowing a trumpet on the stern and elaborate carvings of gargoyles and flowers on the bow. He wondered how sailors were able to find their way from Denmark to the Guinea Coast of Africa without getting lost. He wondered how they kept doing it for hundreds of years. It wasn't as though the sea was a road... and even though his father had explained it over and over again, Kø just couldn't imagine it. Soon, very soon, he would see the chronometer in action. His father had given him an old one when he was about twelve years old, and it was his treasured possession. Whenever his father went back to Denmark for business, Kø would dig it out from its hiding place, and he was comforted by the long absences. Kø was assured that with a chronometer he would always be able to find his father.

"Denmark is in that direction." His father had told him showing him exactly where it was on the map of the world in his office. "If you have a chronometer, you will always find your way to me. And with the chronometer, you can find your way safely to any seaport in the world."

Kø looked from the map to his father and nodded gravely. It meant that they would never be separated, and that was all he needed to know. The way the chronometer worked still didn't make sense to him, but soon, he knew he would understand all those mysteries because he was going to be on *The Pharaoh* the next time it set sail for Denmark.

The wind picked up speed, and the small ripples in the ocean picked up steam. The sea started to change color, and its greyish froth splashed noisily as the tide began to come in. Suddenly, a dolphin streaked out of the ocean, flew in a perfect semi-circle and plunged, nose first, back into the sea. Kø laughed in delight. If his mother ever got to know that he had ridden on the back of that particular dolphin many times, she would have his hide. It didn't matter that he was far taller than she was; she would have chased him with the big paddle she used for cooking 'akple,' the cornmeal staple, for swimming in dangerous waters where the rip current was known to swallow grown men and suck them straight into the unknown vortex of the ocean.

The waves whacked the beach with vigor and the strong wind carried with it the slightly raw smell of the sea, dead leaves from coconut trees and the verdant, musky scent of reed growing on the banks of the lagoon no more than two hundred feet away. The wind grabbed and whipped Kø's hair into his face. He impatiently pushed it out of his eyes. His hair was just a shade or two darker than corn husk. It was long and wavy, a testament to

4

his mixed parentage. Kø smiled his lopsided smile so like his father's smile. He could hear his mother's voice shouting:

"For heaven's sake Kondo Quist, you must have your hair cut! No man should keep his hair that long!" When she called him by his full name, he knew he was in trouble.

An eagle suddenly swooped down and snapped up a tiny crab not even two feet from where Kø lay on his elbow... and he was rudely yanked from his reverie.

"Eva!" he shouted suddenly springing into sitting position.

"Heavens help me!!" he muttered. "I'm in trouble! Big trouble!!"

He looked around wildly, trying to gather his thoughts and his belongings, which were scattered about in the sand. He had totally forgotten about Eva. He was supposed to meet her earlier that afternoon. Snatching up his miniature ship with one hand, and his long-forgotten sandals with the other, he turned and ran barefoot in the direction of Eva's house. His bare toes gripped the sand and sent it flying out behind him. His long, wavy hair streaked behind him like the rays of a spectacular sunset.

He arrived at Eva's house, broad chest heaving, trying to smile his charming, lopsided smile while taking in huge gulps of air. Eva was leaning against a wall. One hand was on her hip while she tapped the wall impatiently with long graceful fingers. Frowning, she straightened when she saw him running towards her.

"You!" she said jabbing an accusing finger at the hard muscles of his stomach when he finally screeched to a halt in front of her. She was tall herself, but he was so much taller, that it was easier to jab him in the stomach than in his chest.

"I know, Eva, I know...."

He tried to embrace her awkwardly with his miniature ship in one hand and his sandals in the other, but she moved away from his embrace.

"I've been..." she started.

"...waiting, worried and angry," he completed her sentence, smiling, trying to take the sting out of the hurt he knew she was feeling.

"I know. I'm so sorry, Eva..."

"You were gazing at *The Pharaoh* again"

"You know me too well... It won't happen again."

"Says who?" she asked. Her dimples peeked at him, and suddenly, they laughed together; all tension broken.

Kø pulled a low backless kitchen stool and slouched against the trunk of the almond tree in the middle of the compound. Stretching his long legs in front of him, he rested the miniature ship on a low table nearby.

He smiled deeply into her eyes and said simply, "I made this for you, Eva..."

She lifted the miniature ship and marveled at the superb craftsmanship. Indeed, it was an exact replica of The Pharaoh. The wood had been polished with care till it shone. Every detail was featured from bow to stern.

Kø stitched all twenty-seven sails on the miniature himself with a needle and thread which he had borrowed from his mother's sewing kit. He had cut the sails from calico.

He painted the red cross of the Danish flag, *The Dannebrog*, onto a bit of calico and secured it on the highest mast. It was perfect! That ship was synonymous with Hans Quist, Kø's father. He had left Quitta four years earlier just before Kø turned twenty. Kø had expected him to come back because of the special bond between father and son, but he never did. For a year, Kø was inconsolable. He tried to accept that that was the way so many European men behaved with their African wives and children, but he just couldn't shake off the feeling of abandonment. Deep in his eyes was a pang of sadness that was becoming a part of him.

Eva wished she could somehow erase the hurt. She had tried. God knew she had really tried! Her heart bled for him, but there was nothing she could do. She stood up deliberately and took the miniature ship in one hand. She stretched out the other hand and beckoned him. When he stood up, she gave him the embrace she had refused to give him earlier on. She squeezed him tight, released him and squeezed him tighter again and again.

The two of them had an unusual relationship. Words didn't seem to matter much. They seemed to understand each other's thoughts and moods and somehow finished each other's sentences. The only thing she didn't understand was why he wouldn't commit to marrying her. She had waited patiently for almost three years, and at twenty-two, she was ready to settle down. He was twenty-four and, in her opinion, he should have been her husband, and they would have had a child together by now. With their arms around each other, Eva led Kø to her bedroom on the far side of the compound. They walked in tandem as though walking towards a common goal. Kø looked at Eva when they arrived in the room. She set the ship reverently on a table beside her bed and looked back at him. She had big round eyes with long thick lashes. He understood the question in them.

"And your parents?" he inquired.

"It's market day; they won't be back till late...very late," she said softly. She hung her head one side shyly.

He opened his arms, and she stepped into his embrace. Kø stared at this beauty who was his and his alone. She was like an ancient goddess. Everyone said the gods had favored her with everything a woman would want. She was tall... no, statuesque. Her skin was smooth and dark, like highly polished ebony. She had the grace of a queen. Her dimples were deep and spontaneous, and Kø smiled whenever he saw them. When she spoke, her husky, melodious voice made Kø's heart sing.

He lowered her gently onto the bed.

In the distance, the rustling of the reed and the swooshing of coconut leaves died down to a whisper. They seemed to be waiting...listening. Eva undid the buttons of his shirt while he undid the knot of her skirt. She undid the buttons of his trousers. And he undid the three buttons that held her shirt together. Her breasts were heavy and full. The nipples pointed upwards. He looked down at them. They beckoned him, and he feasted greedily. She came alive, and her fingers found his manhood. She stroked with both hands, and he circled her ample bottom with both hands and squeezed. She moaned. He groaned. Suddenly, they were all over each other. Hands, mouths, breast to chest; his length hard, her sheath warm. The last pieces of her underwear were ripped off, and Kø spread her wide. She was hot and ready. He entered her slowly, savoring her. Kø lost himself in her ecstasy and joined his mouth to hers, swallowing their bittersweet cries. She writhed restlessly under him and stilled only when he buried his long length into her.

Somewhere in the background, the wind gathered speed again and rudely rustled the leaves. Kø sank into Eva again and again. She wrapped her long legs around him and raised her hips to meet him. They sang the eternal song of lovers and clung and separated only to meet again and again till Eva started to implode. The shudders started from deep within her and when Kø plunged into her again, she erupted into her orgasm and detonated all around him shouting his name in one long wail. Her orgasm gripped him, and he exploded into her. He wanted to call out her name, but somehow, he could only manage the last syllable.

"Aaaaaaaah," he groaned.

"Oh, Eva..." he whispered, when he was finally able to separate himself.

"Kø," she said gazing up at him. Love and contentment shone through her eyes. She knew the feeling was mutual.

"Evado," he mentioned her full name after a while. His voice took on a different timbre. There was something in there that she hadn't heard before. She looked at him with a questioning gaze.

"There's something I want to tell you."

"What is it, Kø? What is it?"

"Come, let's go walking."

"At this time of night?"

10

"Please!"

"Where do you want us to go?"

"To my favorite place."

"The beach?"

"Need you ask?"

They laughed as they held hands and took a leisurely walk to the beach. Above them, the night sky was velvet. An enthusiastic artist had sprinkled the night with a thousand assorted stars. The sea was gentle. It lapped the shore with tentative licks, coming and going and doing what it had been doing for millennia. The tide had come in and washed all traces of his being there away. He sat down and pulled Eva down in front of him. She sat with her back to his chest. His body cradled hers. He wrapped his arms around her and shielded her against the cool air. Eva rested her head against his shoulder and relaxed. She blocked out everything except her man, her love for him and the gentle chorus of the sea, the wind, and the rustling leaves dancing in the distance.

"Eva," he spoke directly into her ear, his voice low and deep and she shivered.

"Do you believe in destiny?"

The question was so unusual that she tried to turn to look at him, but he held her firmly in place. In the distance, she could see the ship. Lights shone through some of the portholes. She didn't wonder what was going on. The ship, its contents and the goings on were none of her business. In the distance, some canoes bobbed up and down. She could see their white triangular sails. They seemed to be playing a game of 'now you see me now you don't' because they appeared and disappeared based on the dip and the rise of the waves. Some seemed to be sailing straight toward the ship while others sailed eastward. Those that sailed eastward were fishermen who had gone out to sea. They would be back at the crack of dawn with a bountiful catch of snapper, grouper, anchovies, crabs, shrimps, octopus and all kinds of seafood.

"Destiny?" she asked incredulously... "Destiny???"

"Yes, Eva. Destiny. Do you believe in destiny?"

"I don't know, Kø. I've heard of such things... but I don't know. I've never thought about it. Why? What is it, Kø? Talk to me." This time, she broke away from his embrace and faced him.

He pulled her back into his arms again and pulled her head against him. She looked at the heavens and the stars that filled the sky that night.

"Well, I do, Eva. I believe in destiny."

"Is that what you wanted to tell me? About destiny?" she asked, puzzled.

Maybe he was finally going to talk about marriage, she thought to herself. Her heart skipped a beat. She expected his lopsided smile, but it didn't materialize. Suddenly, she felt a flicker of foreboding. But before it could develop, expand and seize her, Kø started to speak.

"Eva," He said the words slowly as though he had practiced them for a long time and wanted to make sure he didn't leave anything out.

"I've decided to go to Denmark to visit my father."

For the next few seconds, Eva could not find the words to make a retort. Her brain and her mouth refused to coordinate and, in the end, she parroted incredulously:

"You. Have. Decided. To. Go. To. Denmark. To. Visit. Your. Father!"

Kø watched as her emotions played out on her beautiful face: Incredulity, amusement, horror, helplessness and finally, sadness. Tears pooled in her eyes. She looked like a little girl who had just lost her mother. Kø looked away.

"Yes, Eva," he said quietly. He turned toward the ship berthed in the distance, "and the ship I'm going on, is over there...my father's ship, *The Pharaoh*... and Eva," He stopped to take a deep breath. He gathered his courage in both hands and said.

"*The Pharaoh* leaves this weekend, and I intend to be on it."

Eva disengaged herself from him and fell backward into the sand. She looked at the stars intently as though they could answer the many questions she had running in her mind.

13

"But why, Kø, why do you want to go to Denmark?"

"Papi never said goodbye. I want to know why."

"But that's the way all the Europeans that come here behave. Don't you know that? Don't you know that all their families, not only here in Quitta, but in all the Guinea Coast are temporary?"

"I know that. But Papi was not just my father. He was my best friend, my mentor, my hero," Kø paused. When he continued the pain in his voice was palpable.

"And he left.... Just like that! And since he left, something in my life seems to be incomplete, unfinished."

"What, Kø? What could be unfinished with you? You have everything a man could possibly need! You have house, your own business as a carpenter, money... what else do you need? Ah yes,

I forgot this one... your mother is a wealthy woman, and you will one day inherit everything. What else do you want, Kø?"

He answered her question with another question of his own.

"Who am I, Eva?"

"What do you mean?"

"Am I white or black?" he asked her. "Am I my Danish father's son or my African mother's son?"

"You must know you are both, my love. You are Kø. Loving son, responsible, kind, handsome and the love of my life." She listed his attributes on all five fingers.

Eva took both his hands in hers and said earnestly:

"Just be the best you can possibly be, and you will grow into the man you want to be."

She tried to embrace him, to somehow soothe the pain in his voice, but he held her back.

"Then why do people here call me *Yevu*[2]? And yet my step-brothers call me *Sortsøn*[3]."

"What was the relationship with your father like?"

"I knew that I was his son. I loved him, and I believed he loved me"

"Then let that be enough for you, Kø." she urged.

"But he left without a word, without a backward glance. When I was little, I used to follow him everywhere he went, and he wouldn't go anywhere without me. People used to call me his shadow. Before I met my step-brothers a few years ago, I really thought I was his only son. His only child."

Kø paused, and when he resumed, his voice was filled with pain.

"He told me, that I looked so much like him when I was born, that he named me after himself. Was his love real, Eva? Was I just a product of trade? Was I just an inconvenient shadow?"

---

[2] Literal meaning is 'sly fox'. Refers to a white person in the Ewe language.

[3] Danish for black son.

15

The silence that hung between them after Kø's question was laden and heavy. Even the noisy waves nearby couldn't fill the silence.

"Oh, Kø," Eva cried suddenly, "I don't want you to be captured and sold into slavery. Have you considered that our people are sold slavery?"

"No-one would sell me. Not everyone is sellable, you know. Besides the slave trade was abolished a long time ago."

"Please, Kø! Please, don't go!" she pleaded with tears in her eyes.

"What will happen to us? What about me? What about our future? I'm so scared, Kø. Please take your father out of your mind. He is gone. He gave you what he could. Don't force him to give you more. Don't risk your freedom!"

She looked at him imploringly:

"It's better to eat mushrooms in freedom than to eat meat in slavery."

"That is true, Eva ..." said Kø thoughtfully, "however, they also say, 'He who asks questions can't lose his way.' I must have my questions answered, and I promise to accept any outcome. I have made my decision to go, Eva. But one thing I promise you is that I will be back; we will be married, and we will be together. I believe in destiny, my love, and I believe that what is written is written."

Kø lay down in the sand and pulled the sobbing Eva into his arms. He wrapped his arms around her and hugged her hard.

"I will come back to you, Eva. I promise!" he whispered intently over and over again.

He continued to hug her till her sobs subsided. He stroked her lush bottom and savored her curves. He etched the soft angles and the alluring curves of her figure in his mind as he stroked her. He pressed her breasts against his chest. Her breath was warm and tickly against his neck, and he found himself stirring again. His hands wandered down to her behind again. He squeezed and pressed her close till her pubis made contact with his cock. The sea played its seductive song. He put his feet between her legs and spread them wide. Her quiet crying turned into a gasp. His tongue played with hers. He unfastened the knot on her skirt again and slipped her panties to one side. He touched her in her innermost part, and Eva lifted herself from her lying position. When she raised herself, he positioned himself to fill her. His thumb found her most sensitive spot and fondled it gently. When they climaxed again that night, they emitted the combined sounds of wonder, fulfillment, sorrow and hope.

2

The Fort, March 6th, 1850

The Quist brothers, Harald, Herbert and Hugo, had just finished having their dinner with a dozen or so very important visitors in the formal dining room of The Fort. The dinner was extremely successful. As usual, Metrova, who cooked everything, had outdone herself. Just as she looked after her husband, Hans' personal and business concerns, she also looked after her stepson's concerns.

Denmark had sold all its holdings in the Guinea Coast[4] to the United Kingdom for ten thousand pounds, and the dinner was a final meeting between the old and the new administrations. Present at the handing over dinner was Governor Bray, the British Governor, who was eager to take over from where the

[4] Guinea is a traditional name for the region of the **West African Coast** which lies along the **Gulf of Guinea**.

Danish had left off. General Sønne, who was appointed by the Danish Crown, to document and sell the forts, castles and all their assets and holdings on the Guinea Coast, was there with his pretty wife, Katie. Katie's father was Norwegian, and her mother was half Danish and half *Ga*[5]. She was so light skinned and blue eyed that no-one would have guessed that she had any African blood in her.

Mr. Baeta and Mr. Quainoo, businessmen of Afro/Portuguese descent, were there with their local partners, Mr. Klu and Mr. Adu. They had brought over the last consignment of gold, diamonds, elephant tusks, palm oil and coffee to be sent to Denmark.

The Captain of *The Pharaoh*, and trusted, longtime friend of Hans Quist, Captain Laarsen, was invited for dinner. He would oversee the safe loading of all the goods onto the ship before they set sail in the morning.

The dinner had been most successful. Metrova, Kø's mother, had made them a four-course meal fit for a king. The first course was a chowder made from scratch. How she managed to make

---

[5] The Ga are an ethnic group that lives primarily in the **Greater Accra, Eastern Region** and the **Volta Region** of Ghana

garlic flavored croutons to accompany the soup course was something none of the guests could comprehend. The meal was followed by a delicious roast pork, *flæskesteg*, with potatoes and fresh vegetables. The fish for the third course was a delicious grouper baked to perfection. The dessert was *romfromage*. A very thick rum flavored custard made with beaten egg whites with sugar. This was her husband Hans' favorite dessert. She incorporated this into a trifle and topped it with dark, melted chocolate. It was cooled in her icebox, and the chocolate hardened just enough to give the desert the texture it needed. The dessert melted in their mouths on impact. The guests and their hosts savored every mouthful. Harald, the eldest of the three brothers, chose the wine to accompany each course, and the visitors were happy, replete and garrulous.

After all her efforts at preparing the elaborate dinner, Metrova also left a covered platter of *Smørrebrød* - open-faced Danish sandwiches made with *Ribbensteg*, thin slices of roast pork with crackling on the sideboard just in case anyone wanted a snack in the middle of the night.

Harald and his brothers hated to refer to Metrova as their stepmother, however, they understood their father's indiscretions. After all, all three of them had wives and children in Denmark, yet, they also took African wives. It was understood that taking African wives was not only necessary for the survival of European men, it was imperative. The women took care of them, provided much-needed companionship, helped cure them of malaria and other diseases that had killed many of their peers and colleagues. It was also great for business to have alliances with women from powerful families on the coast. In the African mind, there was no alliance more powerful than a marriage alliance. The brothers ensured that neither their mother, Jacoba, nor their own wives ever got to find out about their fathers' or their indiscretions.

The guests were up till one in the morning when they begged to retire to be able to finish their last-minute preparations before leaving for their various places of abode the following day. Kø himself wasn't invited to the dinner, but the news his brothers received about him, later that night, caused every one of them tremendous indigestion. While their guests slept, four men huddled on the upper parapet of The Fort. They didn't want to be overheard.

In the distance, the sea crashed viciously onto the shore, clawing relentlessly at the shoreline, tearing at bits of rock and sand and pulling everything that was loose back into the sea. It was very windy, and the wind threatened to carry their voices if they weren't careful. So, they huddled together even closer and spoke in whispers.

"Kø asked to go to Denmark with us," began Captain Laarsen.

"That's not going to be possible!" exclaimed Harald.

"Of course not!" Herbert answered angrily.

"He must be out of his mind!" Hugo said agreeing with everyone.

"Well, though he asked permission from me," said Captain Laarsen, "he is really coming with us because of this."

The three brothers peered down at the contents of the telegraph Captain Laarsen produced. It was sent from their father to Captain Laarsen. Herbert slowly read out its contents.

MAKE.SURE.YOU.BRING.MY.SON.HANS.KONDO.QUIST.

WITH.YOU.WITHOUT.FAIL.SIGNED. HANS. PIETER. QUIST

Captain Laarsen stood a little apart from the three brothers and digested their incredulity.

"Kø is coming with us on Friday!" he said in a low matter-of-fact voice.

They laughed, uncertain, muted, nervous laughter. Try as they might, they couldn't understand why their father would want his 'bastard' son in Denmark. The fantastic meal was long forgotten. They looked at one another thinking how incredulous that would be. What would their mother think? How would she feel?

Herbert set his wine glass down with a hard thud. The base splintered. The brothers didn't notice as blood dripped from his fingers onto the concrete floor of the parapet.

"He may come with us just because father says so," said Harald, "but we shall say nothing about this telegraph to Kø."

"Every great dream

begins

with a dreamer."

Harriet Tubman

3

Copenhagen, Spring, 1819

Hans Quist was an exceptionally handsome man of twenty-seven, and he knew it. He was tall and golden blond, and he stood at six feet six inches by the time he was seventeen. All the young women who saw him, said the new style of coat and waistcoat were purposely designed to fit his broad shoulders and emphasize his slim waistline. His breeches showcased his long legs and muscular thighs to full advantage. The old women ogled when he passed them by, and when he smiled his lopsided smile, they clutched their shawls tightly around their shoulders and remarked that it was a sin for a man to look so beautiful.

His eyes were the color of the sea in the early hours of the morning: an intriguing blue-green color. His moustache only enhanced sensuous lips. One corner of his mouth was tilted upwards because of a childhood injury. Instead of detracting from his appeal, it looked like he had a permanent semi-smile that held sensuous secrets that no-one in the world was privy to. Hans had a secret alright. It was a secret he held close to his heart since he discovered that the smells of rotting fish gut and horse manure were an indelible mark of poverty. No matter how much one scrubbed, the smell stuck like a louse that had burrowed deep into one's skin.

Hans' father started out as a fisherman when he was much younger. However, he turned to farming when the King allotted land for farming. The King helped farmers with land, seeds and other inputs so that they could feed the new factories Denmark was building to implement and boost the Kings' Industrialization Agenda. Hans' father, Pieter, was happy for the King's assistance and opportunity to serve his nation.

Hans, on the other hand, wanted none of it. His secret was simple. He wanted to make money. No...that was wrong...really, Hans wanted to be rich. Very rich. As rich as the legendary Croesus. His ambition was to walk in the corridors of power. He wanted to be able to walk into the palace at Copenhagen, to have the ear of the King and to be an intrinsic part of Denmark's powerful aristocracy.

If anyone had known this plan, they would have laughed him to scorn. How does the son of a fisherman get such foolish, audacious and grandiose ideas? Hans smiled...a genuine smile this time. He had learned long ago not to share his ambitions with anyone. His solution to his temporary lack of finances, as he put it, was as clear as day and as easy as pie. He was simply going to marry into money. It would take confidence, a great deal of self-education on the finer things of life, and a certain 'je-ne-sais- quoi' which Hans felt he already had.

In his childhood, Hans Quist was a voracious reader though he had only basic education. He found out very early in life that his father couldn't teach him much because he didn't know much. So, he made it a point to read anything and everything. Above all, he made it a point to listen. He acted rather than reacted. He believed in people's inner divine light of reason, and to him, it was important that people use both their senses and their intellect. He believed that the universe would bring him what he wanted and what he deserved, and it had to be good.

Ludvig Holberg and Søren Kierkegaard were his favorite authors. From Holberg, Hans formed his worldview. To him, neither the church nor the state could hold him back in his views. He was a man who believed in liberty, tolerance and progress. Kierkegaard once said: "Once you label me, you negate me", Hans didn't want to be labeled in any way. He believed life was important and was meant to be lived to the fullest. Every day, he thought about Kierkegaard's quote about life: "Listen to the cry of a woman in labor at the hour of giving birth - look at the dying man's struggle… and then tell me whether something that begins and ends thus could be intended for enjoyment." Hans decided to create his own destiny with all seriousness, and so, he mapped out his strategy and set out to do just that.

There was a certain Jacoba Boresen whose picture Hans had often seen in the newspapers. It was a good thing he went to the library to read the papers every day. He couldn't afford the luxury of purchasing them, but by reading them, he kept abreast with everything that happened nationally and also internationally Jacoba was no great beauty, but she was tall, lithe and had a wonderful figure. From the pictures, she seemed to have a luscious bosom, and that was good enough for Hans.

Jacoba had just turned twenty-one, and she had just come into an astronomical inheritance that her grandmother, the King's cousin, twice removed, had left her. Judging from the number of soirees she attended, chaperoned by her parents, it was evident that they were looking for a suitable husband for her. Well, they would soon find that he, Hans, was just the right man for her. He wasn't going to take her money and run, that was beneath him. He was simply going to use her money to make more money. There were few things he agreed with in the Good Book, but the one thing he totally agreed with was that "Money answers all things." And yes, there was one other thing he agreed with... that "He who finds a wife, finds a good thing." Hans decided he was going to marry Jacoba; he had it all planned out. The best time to meet her was on Easter Sunday. The church that she and her family attended was the Lutheran Church of Denmark, which was located in Kalundborg, about sixty miles east of Copenhagen.

Every Easter, in Kalundborg, a wealthy family sponsored a fête on Resurrection Sunday. It was one of the two days of the year that nobility and the plebiscite mingled without the invincible barrier of wealth. The other day was Christmas Day. This year, according to the newspaper article, the Boresen family was sponsoring the Easter festivities. Hans had no intention of waiting until Christmas Day when Easter was barely two weeks away.

On Wednesday, April 7th, 1819, Hans left his family home in Copenhagen to begin his journey to Kalundborg. He wore his one good peplum styled coat with a high collar, starched cravat, blue and gold brocaded waistcoat, highly polished musketeer boots, and a beautiful broad hat complete with a white feather. He restyled his beard to the new pointy *Van Dyke* style and allowed his golden blond hair to curl and hang loosely around his shoulders. He checked and re-checked his money- it was money he had won from a lucky night of gambling. It was enough for a week's stay and nothing more.

The grueling three-day coach journey didn't bother him. The leaves on the trees were young and tentative, as if they were afraid of what the cold would do to them if they bloomed too quickly. The wild flowers and yellow tulips were boldly beginning to bloom - a sure sign that spring had arrived. However, the air was still nippy - the cold hands of winter still refused to relent its grip on the land. Hans clutched his greatcoat tightly around himself and stared unseeing out of the window. All he thought about was that, on Easter Sunday, the stars would align in his favor and his future would begin.

Marriage is like a peanut,

you have to crack it

to see what is

inside...

Ghanaian proverb

4

Resurrection Sunday, 1819

Jacoba was dressed in a fashionable, pale lilac day gown. Her hair missed being called blond, and neither was it a deep rich brown. It reminded Hans of weak tea with very little milk in it. Her hair, though nondescript in color, was lush and thick. It was styled with masses of curls stylishly placed over her forehead and ears. At the back, the hair was drawn up into a loose Grecian inspired *Psyche Knot.*

She looked sweet and innocent as she sat between her parents on the front row pew of the Lutheran Church in Kalundborg. Hans sat about ten seats diagonally behind them. He heard nothing the priest said that day, rather, he studied Jacoba's profile intently. She was very photogenic indeed, he decided. It was as though an indecisive sculptor had caused her to miss the description "pretty." However, her bosom was ample and her money even more so. Hans' mouth watered. He wasn't sure whether it was from looking at her bosom or from the money that would soon be his. Both, he decided, would make an ambitious, hot-blooded man's mouth water.

Finally, the service was over, and the fête began. There was music, food and drink in abundance. The first course was pickled herrings, prawns, hardboiled eggs, tuna, liver pate and various cold cuts. The warm dish came second, and according to tradition, it contained lamb, eggs and chicken. Beer and schnapps were in abundance. Hans decided to touch neither food nor drink. He waited patiently until all the introductions were over. Then he waited till Jacoba moved away from her parents to get herself a drink and something to eat. He moved swiftly and stood right behind her.

"*Vil du danse med mig*?" He asked, "Will you dance with me?"

Startled, she turned around swiftly to face the voice. She looked in Hans' beautiful blue-green eyes and admired his teeth as he smiled his most boyish, most charming, most lopsided smile. The sun shone behind him, turning his golden blond hair into a halo. No matter what Jacoba did, she couldn't find her voice. So, she gave up after several attempts. What she did know with startling clarity was that she was staring into the eyes of the Adonis of her dreams. Jacoba didn't stand a chance against Hans' charm, wit, warmth and humor. He made her laugh and made her feel that she was the best thing since *Æblekage*.[6]

Hans swept her off her feet, and she willingly fell into his arms. He was her constant companion during and after the fête. Three days later, she decided she couldn't live without him. He assured her that he couldn't live without her either. Barely a month after they met, despite misgivings from parents, friends and family, Hans and Jacoba were married.

During the first four years of the marriage, Hans gave Jacoba all the attention and love a man could give a woman. He showered her with gifts and taught his wife the art of *Kama Sutra* and other exotic ways of lovemaking. He gave her great pleasure in the making of three boisterous baby boys. He wanted to make sure that she would be content with being the wife of an absentee husband, mother of three boisterous sons and benefactor through his philanthropic organizations. He wanted to be sure that she wouldn't distract him when he started his 'Great Adventure'. He never forgot though, that it was through her that his dreams would be realized and so, he did everything to

---

[6] A sweet dessert called apple charlotte.

show her how grateful he was. Jacoba was sure that she was the luckiest woman alive.

In the first four years of their marriage, while his wife was getting pregnant, delivering beautiful babies and looking after their three

sons, Hans relentlessly pursued his dreams. He ordered the best wood from Russia and left it for two years to cure properly before using it to build his ship. He then commissioned the best naval architects and shipbuilders in Norway and Germany to design and build the most modern, lightweight and fast merchant vessel. He outfitted his ship with the latest gadgets, including a brand-new version of Harrison's chronometer, which Captain Cook had previously used to circumnavigate the globe. He also included the latest steering devices and added more sails to ensure that the sail time would be much shorter. Hans' ship was an ultra-modern ship that would facilitate trade between Africa, the West Indies, and Europe. It was built with the possibility of jumboizing or making larger just in case trade became lucrative and the need to carry more cargo arose. No expense was spared to decorate the dozen first-class cabins as well as the lounge and dining areas. There were painted murals in each cabin of scenes drawn from Greek and Roman mythology. The bow and the stern were all decorated with intricate carvings of angels, flowers, and dragons.

Meanwhile, Hans joined the Council of Merchants in Denmark, Norway, and Sweden to legitimize himself as a businessman. The King gave him the necessary letters of introduction to the Administration in Africa as well as the West Indies. After four years of hard work, Hans dream ship sailed into Copenhagen harbor. It was sleek and beautiful, two hundred and fifty feet long and fifty feet wide and could carry six hundred tons of goods. It was not only an engineering marvel, but an art piece as well, and when the wind filled all twenty-six sails, Hans' heart threatened to burst with pride. He had invested a great deal of money in goods for sale including arms and ammunition, schnapps and other drinks, fabric and cheap jewelry. Of course, some of the ammunition was to be used to protect his considerable investment just in case unfriendly ships and pirates were tempted to attack. He personally oversaw the *lolo* or loading operations of all the goods himself.

Finally, Hans completed all formalities and paid the "sound dues," the 2% tax on all his goods as requested by the Danish Crown. His heart was filled with wonder and gratitude when he waved his family goodbye. His parents stood a little apart from his wife, his three sons and his wife's family. Their eyes, round as twin moons and their mouths formed into a lax, semi-permanent 'O' as they gazed in awe at their son's incredible achievements.

It was only when Hans rang the ship's bell to mark the beginning of his adventure, the beginning of his new life, and the beginning of the fulfillment of his dreams, that he felt he was now a man. The man he always wanted to be. As *The Pharaoh* sailed away, Hans saw the Danish coastline become smaller and smaller. Then he turned and faced the ocean. The gentle winds favored the journey. The sails were full. Hans faced his future and refused to look back.

"*Life can only be understood backwards,*

but it must be lived

forwards."

Søren Kierkegaard

5

November, 1824

It was the humid, cloying, equatorial heat and reddish, hazy, harmattan air that indicated to Hans, Captain Laarsen and all on board that they were finally nearing Quitta. Hans and Captain Laarsen were in the captains' lounge filling in the muster logbook in which they kept records of the details of the trip. Hans was drinking *aquavit*, the alcoholic bitters recommended for dealing with sea sickness and stomach maladies. After sixty-two days of sailing, Hans' stomach was consistently unsettled. Captain Laarsen, the captain of the ship, who was a veteran sailor, settled for a small glass of mead[7].

"We should be near the coast of Quitta in the next day or so," said Captain Laarsen.

"It's about time," said Hans grumpily.

[7] Mead is one of the world's oldest alcoholic beverages

It had been long days of anticipation. Sometimes it was plain sailing. The sea was a vast expanse of ever-changing colors and ever-changing hues. Its surface unpredictable, its depths simply unfathomable. From time to time, a school of dolphins would leap out of the depths and plunge back in, entertaining the sailors. Hans was grateful that the availability of money meant he could create the best form of transportation known to man to carry him over the expanse of water.

The words "Land Ahoy!" finally rang in Hans' ears like a triumphant symphony. The ship's watchstander was agog with excitement as were all the sailors on board. He saw land in the distance from his superior position on top of the mast long before anyone else and Captain Laarsen grabbed a pair of binocular instruments and indeed, in the distance, was land!

The fishermen who were dragging in their nets stopped mid-drag and squinted at this new ship. The fisherwomen had put their basins upside down in the sand. They sat on them and gossiped as they braided each other's hair, waiting patiently for the day's catch to come in. A few of them munched on *agbelikaklo,* a chewy, grated coconut biscuit. Their children loitered around, playing imaginary games and chasing tiny translucent crabs. As if in slow motion, their attention was riveted to the huge ship that berthed in the distance. A smaller boat carried about a dozen people and samples of everything the sailors had brought.

A statuesque young woman stood akimbo and watched the boat as it neared the shore. She wore a long, patterned skirt and a matching blouse. On one of her wrists were several gold bangles and on the other wrist were several keys hanging from chains. She had gold ornaments in her hair and a combination of beads and gold on her ankles. She was surrounded by about a dozen muscled men. They flexed their glistening muscles. The harvest of fish was long forgotten. The young woman looked fearless, proud and beautiful. It was obvious she was no ordinary fisherwoman. She whispered something to one of the men, and he went running into town. Everyone else waited as the boat carrying Hans and his men came to shore waving their white flags. Everyone understood it was the universal sign of non-aggression. Behind the woman and her "bodyguards" was a crowd, growing larger by the minute. Undoubtedly, the curiosity of the townsmen had been piqued by an alarm that had just been sounded.

Considering that Hans was six feet six inches tall, the woman stood at just about half a foot shorter. Piercing black eyes met piercing blue-green eyes. Something sizzled. Hans knew then that he had just met the other very important woman in this next phase of his life. Here was a woman who would introduce him to her brother, the King of Quitta. With her support, he would build The Fort which became his commercial base for almost three decades. This was a woman through whose influence he would establish his business which would extend to cover almost two-thirds of the African continent. With her expert business sense and invaluable knowledge of local and regional politics, Hans became so successful at his business that he traded as far as Mauritania and the Sudan, as far east as Nairobi and as far south as Zambia. In return, he purchased elephant tusks for ivory, gold, diamonds, bauxite and palm oil and shipped them to Denmark. He bought sugar, rum, and molasses from the West Indies and he set up factories in Denmark that manufactured jewelry, baked goods, and liquor which he exported to the rest of Europe from the United Kingdom all the way to Russia.

On that beach on that day in December 1819, Hans met the woman who would give him another son, his fourth son, Hans Quist II. Metrova became his wife, his lover, his friend, and partner in every way possible. When she gave birth to their only son, she gave him his middle name 'Kondo.'

"He needs to have a name that I can relate to," she told Hans. "He will have to straddle Europe and Africa, Copenhagen and Quitta," she continued. "And he will need to know, that he belongs in both worlds completely and must be rooted in both worlds completely."

Through their union, a part of Hans' heart would be left in Africa forever. His seed would forever be rooted in the African soil. Not even the fickle, ever-shifting sands of Quitta could erase his name. His progeny would continue for generations to come.

6

May 10th, 1850

There was absolutely no fanfare when the Quist family, their staff and the final group of thirty-three members of Danish administration left the shores of Africa on the morning of May 10th, 1850. They had come to the Guinea Coast unannounced and uninvited. They took what they wanted and left behind what they didn't want or couldn't take. And they left unannounced and unheralded.

The English had already set up their administration at the Cape Coast Castle which was situated about four hours away. For some reason, they preferred that Castle to the Christiansborg castle in Accra, which was where the Danes had previously set up their administration. So, despite the hangover from the festivities of the previous night, Governor Bray, left at the crack of dawn to begin the all-important business of Colonization. The bi-color Danish flag had been removed and the tri-color flag of Great Britain was flying high on top of the Cape Coast Castle. They firmly put their stamp of ownership on the region: They promptly changed the Danish reference of the land from "The Guinea Coast" to "The Gold Coast." Duty called most urgently!

The Danes had been in what they called the Guinea Coast since 1658. For one hundred and ninety-two years, they traded slaves, gold, silver, diamonds, drinks, and ammunition among other things. The Quist family had been in Quitta for the last thirty years. One would have thought that their departure would have been heart-wrenching since their presence was firmly rooted in the golden sand. They were leaving behind their buildings, their language, their education, their schnapps, which had become an intrinsic part of the West African culture, and hundreds of half Danish children.

Their departure made no difference to the people of Quitta. To them, one batch of foreigners was trading places with another batch. The Portuguese came and went, then the Germans, Swedes, Dutch, Norwegians, the Danish and now the English had arrived with their stiff upper lips, their tea drinking manners and a different uniform for the governor. The people reckoned that when they had their fill of whatever it was that they wanted, they would also leave. So, the villagers went about their business as usual.

If Hans Quist had been there that day, he most certainly would have felt the agony and anxiety of separation. He had spent much more time with Metrova, Kø's mother, and the son from their union than he did with his wife and sons back in Denmark. Both women had played a major role in his success in life. Jacoba opened the door, and Metrova made the way.

A small band of people stood in the sand, weeping. Metrova and her sisters wept silently. The women were somberly dressed in the darkest brown they could find. They couldn't wear black because they were not mourning a death. So, they stood there unadorned and barefoot with headscarves worn over low their foreheads and ears as a symbol of their anguish. Beside Metrova, stood her brother, the King of Quitta and his entourage. The men were colorfully dressed in full regalia - bold patterned hand-woven Ewe *Kente*[8] worn toga-style. Underneath the toga, they wore collarless white shirts called 'jumpa.' The 'togas' or shorts

---

[8] Kente (aka Kete) is the most famous and the most celebrated of all the textiles used in Ghana. Kente is woven on a horizontal strip loom, which produces a narrow band of cloth about four inches wide. Several of these strips are carefully arranged and hand-sewn together to create a cloth of the desired size.

worn under the *Kente* were made of velvet which the European merchants had sold to them. The shin-length 'togas' were comfortable and roomy and allowed for much-needed ventilation. A young teenage boy held a large multi-colored umbrella under which the king stood.

The priest from the Lutheran mission was there in his long white robe, looking like a tired angel. He looked at the images sewn into the king's ornamental umbrella and wondered what the images meant. He had seen the umbrella many times before but had never asked. He sighed inwardly and piously carried his large well-thumbed bible in both hands as he walked slowly to join the group waiting at the beach. He wondered whether his evangelical work would ever be completed. His worn sandals showed that he had walked the length and breadth of the towns and villages in the area, trying to evangelize hard-headed heathens.

The Chief of Quitta opened a bottle of the schnapps the Danish traders had left him and poured out a libation:

> *Mawuga sogbolisa, kitikata,*
> *amesi wɔ dzifo kple anyigba,*
> *Aɖaŋtɔ be yɛ wɔ asi kple afɔ.*

47

The Supreme Being who is superior to all,
SOGBOLISA, the one who is the embodiment of
Sogbo (masculine) and Lisa (feminine) spirits.
Kitikata the one who created the microcosm (Kiti) from the
macrocosm (Kata).
The one who out of the formless heavens created the earth:
The great and overall God.
The great craft-person who creates hands and feet!

He prayed earnestly as he asked for Kø's safety on the seas and his safe return.

The fetish priest was there, dressed in a long white skirt firmly knotted at the waist. His similarly clad assistants stood beside him with his drums and paraphernalia. He stood as far away from the Lutheran priest as possible. Instead, they ended up facing each other. Amulets surrounded his muscled upper arms, and square leather talismans crudely stitched onto a long leather necklace, hung menacingly around his neck. He held a white horsetail which he swished in the air, from time to time, muttering to himself.

The Lutheran priest raised his eyes to look for hills along the sandy beaches as he recited his favorite psalm, Psalm 121 aloud.

His lips moved rapidly as he recited the prayer in Hebrew, something he hadn't done since he left seminary more than fifty years ago.

"Eisa einai el heharim, me ayin yavo ezri?
Ezri me im ADONAI oseh shamayim va aretz"
"I will lift up my eyes to the hills, from whence cometh my help?
My help comes from LORD, who made heaven and earth."

There were no hills anywhere. The sandy beaches stretched as far as eye could see. He bowed his head and closed his eyes. There, in his mind's eye, he found his source of faith and conjured up the highest of hills.

The sound of drums suddenly resonated through the air, drowning out the sounds of weeping and angst. A sound so primal and deep, it touched the very soul of the hearers. A calling of spirits to attention. Speech without words. Even the winds gathered to listen.

The fetish priest mixed a concoction of water and corn dough in a calabash, stirring it slowly then faster and faster till it swirled in the calabash, creating a translucent vortex. As he invoked his gods loudly, he spoke in ancient rhythm. Rhythm and drum beat perfectly to time. He bent and poured the concoction away

49

from his feet toward the sea, controlling the calabash, so only a small amount of liquid were poured out each time. Then he poured to his left and right. His prayers became a chant of ancient dialogue.

Finally, he turned the calabash toward his feet and poured the rest of the concoction toward his feet as the drum stilled into silence. He reached into the recesses of his white calico skirt and brought out two cowrie shells and talismans.

"Take this, my son," he said to Kø handing him an amulet tied to a cowrie shell, "and tie it around your arm. The gods will protect you! You will come back to us!"

Now it was the Lutheran priest's turn.
"Let us pray," he intoned. He moved away from the fetish priest's line of vision and his brow furrowed deeply as he began to pray.
"Our Father..." he began.
"Who art in heaven, hallowed be thy name..."
Almost everyone there joined him in prayer, genuflected and made the sign of the cross as he said his last 'Amen.'

Eva was inconsolable. She threw herself in the sand, rolling and wailing. Kø tried to help her up and wipe the sand off her. It was in her clothes, in her hair, on her face, mixed with tears and snot. He tried to be brave and resolute and hid a helpless tear that appeared at the corner of his eye.

Metrova embraced her only son in a long, tight embrace. Her heart ached, but she understood her son better than anyone did. She understood his need to find his father, and she understood the hazards involved in the mission her son chose to undertake. She was glad that every prayer had been made for his protection. Like her husband, she was a woman who believed in the impossible. She stood tall and proud and resolute, and she lent her only son all her strength.

"Go, Kø, and find your father," She whispered in his ear.

"But as you travel, know that you are not among friends. Speak softly, my son, but carry a big stick and you will go far. Our people say, 'an army of sheep led by a lion can defeat an army of lions led by sheep'. Always remember who you are. You come from a long line of kings, so you are a lion. Stand up for yourself. Fight for what is right and above all, no matter what happens, come back home."

Kø clung tightly to his mother.

"I promise, mother. I will come back."

Meanwhile, a little way away, Harald, Kø's oldest brother was saying goodbye to his "African wife" and their three wide-eyed daughters. His wife was very young, and she had a blank, expressionless look on her face. She refused to look at her husband as he spoke to her, looking this way and that, at times playing with her youngest daughter's braided hair, undoing the neat braids and re-braiding them over and over again. She knew what her fate was, and she was matter-of-fact about it. It was time for the father of her children to leave the country. She would be left to fend for herself and her children. And that was that!

Fortunately for her, there was a hard-working shallot farmer who had promised to marry her and take care of her children once Harald left. The farmer was waiting for her at his stall in the market. As soon as Harald left, she and her children would meet him, so he could take her to their new home. She couldn't hear what Harald was saying. It went through one ear and came out of the other. Harald was wasting her time.

Hugo and Herbert were bored by the whole scene. There was a fortune in the hold of The Pharaoh and getting it to Denmark was paramount in their minds. Everything had been perfectly stored in watertight compartments. Harald, Hugo and Captain Laarsen had supervised the loading of everything themselves. They had loaded carefully, checking and rechecking the weight, making sure that it was in perfect ballast or balance when they were ready to set sail. The cargo was battened down, so it wouldn't move around. They calculated the space needed for the rum, molasses and sugar they intended to pick up from the West Indies and thick heavy chains were placed in the empty holds to make sure the weight was even, or else, the ship would tip and capsize.

.

The brothers had given the King of Quitta some money to ensure that their children were given a good basic Christian education. The children knew they would never visit their fathers and the fathers knew they would never come back. That's the way it had been for the two centuries that Denmark traded on the Guinea Coast of Africa.

It was because of that knowledge, they just didn't understand why their father wanted Kø to visit him in Denmark. Try as they might, they couldn't find a reason for their father's seeming impetuousness. All three brothers eyed Kø malevolently as he finally boarded the canoe that would take them on to *The Pharaoh*. Kø was the last to climb in before the oarsman pushed off. He lost his balance temporarily, and a small hand shot out to steady him. When he looked up, the young woman who steadied him smiled.

"*Woezor*, welcome!" she said smiling. She moved her feet out of the way, so he could sit across from her and her husband.

"Do you speak *Ewe?*" he asked in surprise.

"I do," she said.

Most white women would not deign to speak the local language. He looked into her big blue eyes, and his confusion was total. She said something to him, but the wind carried her voice away. He looked at her with curiosity, and she looked back at him and gave him a mischievous half-smile. Her elderly husband, who wore black boots and the stripes of a general on his uniform, tightened his arms around her and Kø looked away and focused on the sea and the uneven ripples as they headed toward *The Pharaoh*. They were all embroiled in their own thoughts. They thought about the events that led them on this journey, those left behind, the future and what it might hold.

7

General Sønne and Katie married just a month before the journey to Denmark. This was Katie's first trip on a ship, and she was ecstatic when they got to *The Pharaoh*. She almost capsized the canoe in her haste to get onto the ship. The General looked fondly at his wife and was happy with his decision to marry her. She was young, vivacious and sparkled like sparklers at Christmastime. She was just like his first wife, Belle. When she looked up at him adoringly with her big blue eyes, he promised himself that he would love her and protect her in a way he hadn't been able to do with his first wife.

Twenty years earlier, he and Belle arrived on the Guinea Coast to take up his new position as governor. They landed just before the rainy season in 1830 a few weeks after their wedding. Barely a month after they got there, Belle contracted malaria… she had no immunity, and she was dead within a week. The General

55

never got over her untimely death and refused to marry ever again. Not as long as he was on the Guinea Coast! It was only when the Danish administration decided to sell its holdings and leave that he finally decided it was time to find a replacement for Belle. Katie was the perfect choice. She was twenty-two, the same age as Belle was when they first arrived. She was pretty, vivacious and educated enough to fit in with his family and friends back in Denmark. With her big blue eyes, no one would ever suspect that she had any African blood.

The marriage had been arranged by Katie's grandparents and the General's most trusted assistants who had been tasked to find him a suitable wife. The General had considered several other girls, but Katie came with an offer he couldn't refuse.

When Katie's grandparents heard that General Sønne was looking for a wife to take back to Denmark with him, they offered him a very appropriate woman: She was beautiful, elegant, well-mannered and educated. She had auburn hair and blue eyes and would pass for a Danish lady. Katie's grandparents told the General, in confidence, that her deceased parents, Dag and Alfreida, had left her a large inheritance. They offered him all of it if he married her.

Katie smiled when the boat stopped next to *The Pharaoh*. Her heart was light, her sense of adventure heightened. She felt as though a fresh page of her life was now opened waiting to be written. She was sure the pages would be filled with joy, happiness and love.

Gone was life at the ranch with cows mooing and lowing... perpetually munching and perpetually defecating.

Gone was the arid weather in the Northern region. It was so dry at times that it cracked open one's lips, nostrils and the soles of one's feet and caused them to bleed.

Gone was the raw, pungent smell of shea butter which was the only thing emollient and soothing enough to soften stiff, hard skin dried out by the climate.

Gone were people who couldn't come to terms with the fact that she looked white but spoke just like they did.

Gone were the inquisitive looks of the gossips who stopped talking immediately she came close: but always refused to tell her what it was they were whispering about.

Gone were stiff unloving parents she could not relate to.

Gone! Gone!! Gone!!!

She couldn't wait to experience all the new and exciting things life would bring. Now she would have a house in Copenhagen. She would go to soirees, dinners, and dances with her important husband. She would wear the finest silk gowns and wear expensive European perfumes.

Indeed, she was the luckiest girl on the Guinea Coast!

Once they settled in the lavish owner's suite, the General made sweet love to his young wife. She lay on their tousled bed sleeping. He looked at the sweet curve of her lips and sighed contentedly as he lit his cigar. She was his and his alone, and he was going to make sure he took good care of her. It was a pity that her parents had died so tragically. He had made her grandparents tell him everything. That was his one condition for marrying her. He wanted no secrets about her life. He sighed again as he remembered Alfreida and Dag's tragic story.

8

1827

Alfreida was upset! Very upset! She stomped up and down from the verandah to the gate of her parents' home, and back, muttering to herself in anger. Her thick brown pigtails flailed in the air.

Her parents had just announced that they had found her a "suitable" husband. Dag, the prospective husband, was short, stocky and stout with a head full of curly, reddish-gold hair. He was considered handsome when he was a young man, and many girls had fallen in love with his brazen, bad-boy ways. But with time, drink and squinting in the sun at sea, permanent lines etched a sorry story on his face. He had just arrived from Norway and had found himself a lucrative job as a personal assistant to the deputy Governor with the Danish Administrator at the Christiansborg Castle in Accra.

Dag ran away from home at fourteen and decided what better way to see the world than from the tallest mast of a ship. Any ship would do. He signed up with the first ship that would take him on at the harbor in Bergen, the harbor city in Norway. There was no continent he hadn't been to. He had a knack for picking up languages easily and ingratiating himself to his bosses. Though he was Norwegian, he was given a job with the Danish administration, not only because he spoke fluent Danish, having worked on a Danish vessel for several years, but also because he saved an influential Danish merchant from financial fraud. The merchant in question had important connections to the Administration. So, after twenty-seven years of wanderlust, Dag used his connections to find work in Accra, with the intention of making some money, before going home to Norway to settle down with a beautiful, blond Norwegian girl.

He had heard how necessary it was to find himself a girl to settle with while in Accra.

"They know how to keep us alive when sickness comes," his colleagues told him.

"And, boy, they do know how to make a man comfortable!" another said to him.

"Besides, time will pass quickly when you have a companion; before you know it, your time is up!"

"But don't I have to take her back with me if I marry her?" he asked.

"No-one does that!!! **Everyone** leaves their African wives behind!"

"Besides, when you marry one of those mullatoes from a good family, they will open other business connections for you."

"And you can earn even more than the Administration pays you!" another informed him.

One day, after several rounds of drinking *Pito*[9] with co-workers, the name Alfreida came up. He found out where she lived, observed her and really liked what he saw. Alfreida was a beautiful seventeen-year-old. She was slim, had a tiny waist and a pert ass that would easily fit into his beefy waiting hands. She might not have realized it, but she swayed seductively as she walked, and her thick, wavy hair swayed in tandem. She constantly wore it in four pigtails which she adorned with various colored beads to match whatever she was wearing. When the nipples of her pert, young breasts showed through the thin fabric of her blouse, Dag decided she would do him just fine. He had a group of co-workers from the administration approach her parents for her hand in marriage as was the custom. They initially refused because they had heard about his

[9] A locally made alcoholic brew made with millet

drunkenness, but when he doubled her dowry and gave Alfreida's father enough money to live in comfort, her parents readily acquiesced. Dag paid a major part of the three-part dowry, and after much negotiation, her parents requested that he wait for a few months while she finished her basic education. They agreed that immediately she was done, he could pay the rest of her dowry and complete the marriage rites.

Dag promised to wait. But after talking to Alfreida one evening, the sight of her nipples through her thin blouse was too much for him. He hastily turned her against a wall in a dark alley, tore aside her panties and thrust himself rudely into her. In three thrusts he was done. He turned baleful bloodshot eyes to her and said:

"*Min kjære,* my dear," he said licking his lips. "you are so sweet, so beautiful! I wouldn't have done this if you weren't so tempting. I'm so sorry."

"I'm sorry," he apologized again stroking one thick plait that had come undone. "It won't happen again *min kjære.*"

"My name isn't Clara," she said angrily misunderstanding the endearment '*kjære.*' She was shocked and hurt by him.

"You will be my wife anyway so don't worry, baby girl. I will show you how real love is made when we marry."

An unpleasant smell of stale *pito*, and *akpeteshie*[10], oozed from his pores. Alfreida didn't know whether she cried from the pain and humiliation he had inflicted on her when he raped her or from his unpleasant fetid smell. She picked up the tatters of her undergarments and her self-respect and looked at him incredulously. She was sure then that she would never marry this man. With tears running down her face, she held her head high as she stomped away from him.

"I will come and visit you the day after tomorrow," he said to her retreating back.

She walked away without looking back, pigtails swinging madly.

The following day was Christmas Day, and there was a staff party at the Christiansborg Castle. Everyone, including Dag, was drunk or almost drunk from the festivities. The party was everything Dag expected and more, and when it finally ended just after midnight, he picked his way carefully through the dark, cobbled, uneven streets with a bottle of hard-to-find *absinthe* liquor under his arm. He stopped and took a couple of swigs, burped and roared with laughter at the ungracious sound of his burp.

"Another one for the road!" he chuckled. He took a long, satisfying swig and was pleased with the bittersweet taste of licorice, anise and herbs.

---

[10] Alcoholic beverage like rum, made from sugarcane.

He thought about his sweet wife to be, and his desire for her grew with each step. Maybe it was the magical effect absinthe was known to have on the senses. He wasn't sure. He just had to have Alfreida one more time. His trousers felt even tighter as his erection grew at the thought of her. He also wanted to show her that he wasn't a monster. The incident in the alley was unfortunate and not how he planned to have her at all. He decided, in his alcoholic haze, to make it up to her that night. He would make long, sweet love to her and then, he would keep his promise to her parents and wait patiently for the day of their wedding.

Holding the remains of his precious drink tightly under his arm, he stumbled in the direction of Alfreida's house. He decided to take the opportunity that night to really school her in what he expected of her. He grinned at the thought and stopped his tuneless singing long enough to make sure he was on the right road that led to her home. He was. In fact, he was surprised to find that he was right in front of her house.

Alfreida's parent's house was a modest, walled house painted a cheerful yellow. The wall was certainly going to pose a problem because he knew there was no way he was going to be able to scale it. He gave the pedestrian gate a small push and surprisingly, it opened without a sound. He looked cautiously behind him. Then he stretched his short neck and looked into the compound of the house. There was silence everywhere. No movement. In the distance, a dog barked. Another dog answered. Then nothing. Dag tiptoed unsteadily into the house, turning around long enough to push the gate shut without locking it. He then headed in the direction of Alfreida's rooms. Fortunately, her rooms were separate from the main house, so she could come and go without disturbing the household. He thought he heard an unfamiliar sound but wasn't sure. It could have been a sudden wind that rustled the dead leaves that were strewn all over the compound. It was December, and December was harmattan season. The weather was painfully dry as arid winds carried dust and sand particles all the way from the Sahara Desert to the Guinea Coast. The wind dried up everything in its path and left behind piles of dead and dehydrated vegetation in its wake.

Dag peeped through Alfreida's bedroom window to see if he could make out her lithe shape under the blanket. On seeing nothing, he whispered her name and waited. Nothing. He tried the door. It opened at the gentlest touch. Puzzled, he cautiously made his way in, wiping his head and eyes several times as though by doing so, he could lessen the alcoholic haze that still surrounded his head like a squiggly halo.

A sudden movement caught his right eye in the far corner of the room. The four flailing pigtails were very familiar, and he took two or three steps towards them. There, in the throes of orgasm, was Alfreida, totally naked, squeezing her breasts. Her mouth was open, her eyes tightly shut. Her head thrown far back, and she convulsed in ecstasy as she emitted a long, low groan, deep from the recesses of her belly. She was on top of a white man. The man gripped her buttocks tightly as he ground into her. As the man's bare toes began to twitch, he opened his mouth in a silent, sweetly agonizing scream as he joined Alfreida in the culmination of their wild passion. The man was fully clothed from the waist up and totally naked from the waist down. He was wearing a uniform, and Dag just made out the crest on the uniform.

Dag's piercing scream of rage gave voice to the sounds the lovers were desperately trying to suppress. They jumped apart. Clenching his teeth, Dag smashed the bottle of Absinthe on the nearest wall spilling the green liquid all over the place. He was intent on drawing blood, and it didn't matter whose blood it was. He moved like a panther, stealthy, focused and ready for the kill. Alfreida's lover jumped to his feet and pushed her into a corner. His member was thick, hard, and still pulsing from his recent somewhat unfinished encounter. Wild-eyed, he unsuccessfully covered it with both hands and tried to pull the edges of his jacket down further to offer some modicum of decency. He knew he was guilty... very guilty. And he dared not take his eyes off the madman who was his well-known colleague at the Castle.

So intent was Dag on drawing blood from the traitor, that he didn't see the low table in front of him. As he lunged to kill the traitor, he tripped over the stool and fell. The jagged edges of his broken Absinthe bottle pierced his jugular in the process.

Alfreida huddled in a corner. Her eyes were wide and frightened as her husband-to-be bled to death emitting the most fearful, gurgling growls. Each growl pumped blood furiously from his body through the severed vein in his neck. Her lover picked up his pants and ran, leaving her alone to face her fate. Eight hours later that morning, her mother came to find out why Alfreida was still in bed. She found her naked in the same corner her lover had pushed her into, shivering and still looking into Dag's wide-open accusing blue eyes. Alfreida was trapped in the corner by Dag's blackened congealed blood and green sticky semi-evaporated absinthe liquor. By the time her mother reached her, Alfreida was beyond tears and beyond words.

Wracked by scandal, Alfreida's father decided to take his family away from Accra, all the way to Bolgatanga, over 400 miles away, in the Northern part of the country. He bought a huge cattle ranch and settled his family there away from gossip and away from memories. Nine months later, a beautiful auburn-haired daughter, Katie was born. Alfreida took one look at her baby daughter when she opened her eyes. The baby's eyes were just as blue as Dag's eyes had been. All she saw, were Dag's accusing eyes all over again. When Katie was a week old, Alfreida hung herself on a shea nut tree at the remotest edge of her father's property.

Katie's grandparents brought her up as their daughter. They never spoke about her parents, and Katie grew up thinking that her grandparents were her biological parents. They were distant, but they provided everything she needed including an excellent nanny to take care of her.

Her nanny, Ettey, was also of mixed parentage. She had attended the Christiansborg School established by the Danes, and when she graduated, she found a job as an assistant to one of the

Deputy Governor's wives. The lady taught her everything about etiquette and decorum needed by the wife of a high official in a colonial establishment. Katie's grandfather made Ettey an offer she couldn't refuse; so, she stayed and became Katie's pseudo-mother. For twenty-two years, her nanny, Ettey, taught her everything including her own native language, *Ewe*.

General Sønne shook his head as he looked at his wife's slight curves. He put out his cigar, slid under the sheets and put a protective arm around her. She opened her eyes sleepily and snuggled closer to him. By the time the red and white Danish flag, the *Dannebrog*, was hoisted and the anchor pulled up, General Sønne was making love to his wife for the second time that morning.

9

I will never forget the morning we left the shores of my motherland to sail to the shores of my fatherland. Once I entered *The Pharaoh,* I forgot about everyone and everything I had left behind. The knowledge that I would see my father soon was foremost in my mind. It was as though my life was on hold until I saw him and spoke to him. As soon as I set my luggage down, I went to look for Captain Laarsen.

Captain Laarsen and my father had been close childhood friends, and they had worked together for over thirty years. He, I decided, was the best person to teach me everything I wanted to know. I wanted to explore the ship and understand how we could find our way to Denmark over this vast, amorphous ocean. Above all, I just desperately wanted to know how to sail a ship.

The captain was on the quarterdeck. With him, were the watchkeeping officers, the boatswain, and the cook and he was giving orders to everyone. All the other passengers seemed to be in their cabins, so this was a great opportunity for me to put in my request.

"Set the sails for speed!" ordered Captain Laarsen. The boatswain's mates went trotting off to adjust the various sails.

"Boatswain," he said to Johan, the boatswain. "Let me have a copy of the four-hour watches and who is on the look-out. I want to know who is on duty at all times! We need to keep a tight ship here!"

I waited until he finished conferring with staff and issuing his commands.

"Captain Laarsen," I said as I approached him, "I want to help. I can do anything you want me to. I want to learn how to sail the ship. I especially want to know how the compass and the chronometer work. Will you show me?"

The Captain smiled.

"Ja, yes, of course! Junior, I will show you everything." He was the only one who called me Junior because I was named after my father.

"Let's go up to the navigation room first," he continued, leading the way.

"How far is it to the West Indies, Captain?" I asked curiously.

"The journey is three thousand eight hundred and thirty-six nautical miles." Captain Larsen said as we walked along. "And it will take us just under two months to get there."

"And how long will it take to get to Denmark from the West Indies?" I asked eagerly.

"From the West Indies to Denmark would be four thousand two hundred and eighty-five nautical miles!" he answered.

"Then, let me see…. That means it will take us close to three months to get there." I said.

If I waited four years to see my father, I thought to myself, surely, a few more months wouldn't make a significant difference. I was in awe of everything that I saw in the navigation room… the steering wheel, the compass, and the famous Harrisons chronometer!

"The first thing you need to know, Junior, is this," Captain Laarsen said to me as we stood behind the wheel. "You must never forget that you owe a ship all your attention, love, respect and all your skill. Never think that she is just a vessel. If you handle her well, she will serve you well. She will sail with you for as long as she is able to. If you ever neglect or manhandle her, she will leave you on the waves in the middle of a storm."

"I see," I said slowly digesting his words. I would forever keep those words in my mind.

"There are so many things that make the journey by sea difficult, Kø. The wind and the sea are fickle. There's thunder, lightning and strong gales, even hurricanes. The one thing that needs to take us through all that is our ship. If we had manhandled her, she wouldn't be here after thirty years. But she is here with us, sailing with us as though she was a new ship!"

"Don't worry," the Captain said with a smile. "Since you want to know everything, I will teach you everything."

I spent every day from dawn to lunchtime in the navigation room with Captain Laarsen, learning everything about steering, anchoring, navigation and even how to navigate using the stars. I finally understood how highways were made in the ocean using chronometers. Nothing was more fascinating to me!

My brothers seldom went to the navigation room, preferring the comfort of the dining room and its adjacent lounge. There, they drank, played cards, reminisced about life on the Guinea Coast and what the fortune in the ship's hold meant for them. They knew they would never be poor. Their lives were secured for generations to come.

The dining room was most lavishly decorated. I had never seen anything like it. All the furniture was made in rich dark mahogany wood, inlaid with gold. The curtains were made with heavy red velvet, and the candlesticks were made with beaten gold. There were heavy crystal glasses to drink from, and the plates were made of the finest porcelain. All the guests congregated in the dining room or the lounge. I always met my brothers there and apart from a curt nod to my greetings, they hardly acknowledged me. I knew it was wise to steer clear of them.

Katie always came into the dining room with her husband. The General seemed to be very protective of her, and his arm was always around her when they came in. She always smiled at me and everyone else. However, shortly after dinner, she always bade him good night and left for their cabin alone. The General, my brothers and a few of his aides always stayed in the dining room long after the meal was over, smoking cigars and drinking brandy till the sun painted the east in the palest blues and greys of dawn.

There was always a lot of activity on the deck, and I wanted to be part of it.

"It's hard work!" Captain Laarsen said to me when I requested work.

I didn't mind hard work, so he sent me to the chief boatswain to assign me to work and show me everything else I needed to know. The chief boatswain was a ruddy-faced, Danish fellow called Johan. His father used to be boatswain before him; but when his father drowned during a hurricane, on one of their trips back to Denmark, Johan approached Hans and asked for the job, and Hans readily gave it to him. Johan had been working on *The Pharaoh* for the last fifteen years, and he knew **everything** about the ship!

Johan was very muscular and did not have a spare ounce of flesh on him. He had a hard, square jaw that always seemed to have a couple of days' stubble on it. He was almost handsome… but his handsomeness was severely diminished by the way his hair grew in uneven and alarming brown tufts all over his head. Attention was drawn to his erratic hair so much so, that people normally missed his kind eyes and winning smile.

One evening, the ship was on course, and everything was running smoothly. We had just had a good supper and a group number of us relaxed over glasses of aged palm wine that one of the other sailors had smuggled in. We lay on the deck in a semi-drunken state and watched the stars with a deep sense of wellbeing and camaraderie.

"*Skal!*" "Cheers!" Johan said as he settled on the deck of the forecastle with his glass of palm wine.

There was a chorus of cheers in response as we toasted one another and helped ourselves to more highly fermented, delicious palm wine. Most of the sailors were Danish, and as we toasted, they sang the popular Scandinavian drinking song, *Helan Går*. The song is normally sung when people are about to drink *akvavit* or vodka. It wasn't vodka, but palm wine was good enough! Before long, the deck filled with various off-beat versions of the song:

Helan går

Sjung hopp faderallan lallan lej

Helan går

Sjung hopp faderallan lej

Och den som inte helan tar[*]

Han heller inte halvan får

Helan går

(Drink)

Sjung hopp faderallan lej

Here's the first

Sing "hup fol-de-rol la la la"

Here's the first

Sing "hup fol-de-rol la la"

He who doesn't drink the first

Shall never, ever quench his thirst
Here's the first
(Drink)
Sing "hup fol-de-rol la

Johan was on his fourth or fifth shot, and when I was sure he was nice and mellow, I asked him what the cause for his awkward hair growth was.

"Du er for nysgerrig! Lad mig være i fred! "You are too inquisitive! Leave me alone!" he said laughing.

He rubbed a hand over his unruly hair, and it stood on end, giving him a comic quality.

"What happened to your hair, Johan?" I persisted. "What happened?"

"Do tell us what happened!" a sailor said.

"We always wondered what happened to you!" another said.

We hounded him and teased him until he told us the story.

Johan was born with a head full of hair like everyone else. When he was about three or four years old, he got a bad bout of chicken pox. The pox was everywhere, especially on his head and he scratched till his head began to bleed. An old lady swore that she had an herbal remedy which would cure the pox in no time. His mother, in her desperation, bought the remedy which she promptly applied to all the spots. Indeed, the remedy burnt the spots. It worked so well that it burnt the roots of his hair as well!

Johan, the chief boatswain, became my best friend on *The Pharaoh,* and because of him, I became an expert boatswain's mate, and I loved every minute of it. It gave me purpose, and I felt more than ever that beyond being a son, I could be an asset to my father.

Johan showed me everything he knew about ships, and in the seven weeks that we sailed toward the Caribbean, I learned everything about keeping the vessel on course and staying away from danger. I learned how to avoid a collision with other ships. I could navigate the ship with the chronometer and the compass. I learned all there was to know about building, managing and sailing a ship. I learned about knots, hitches, and bends, and I knew how to operate the ships windlasses for letting go and heaving up the anchors.

Johan taught me how to observe the stars to steer a ship without a compass or a chronometer, and I learned how to read the direction of the winds and the currents. I learned how to shoot if we were attacked by any enemy ships. I learned to repair and fix sails when the need arose and took part in the four-hour watches. I kept watch in cold weather and in the heat and was put on the roster along with the other sailors.

I loved everything about sailing, and the hustle and bustle made the time pass quickly. But I loved it the most when I was assigned to be a lookout to observe for any hazards. I loved the sea and the way it pushed back the horizon from the 80-foot height of the mast when I had a 360-degree view. I loved the blackness when the inky sky colluded with the inky sea to cocoon us into a cave of nothingness.

In the evening, the moon was almost always there...sometimes it let in just a sliver of light, in which case, we definitely needed the light from the poop lantern[11]. At those times, the sea seemed to be deceptively without depth and the sky deceptively without height. And sometimes the moon overtook the night and shone so much so that it revealed nature in all its nightly majesty. At other times, black clouds hid the moon from sight, and suddenly, you had a good idea of what it meant to be blind.

I loved sailing when we were alone with nothing but blue sea, blue sky and fickle, amorphous ever-changing clouds in the heavens. Yet in the space and limitless expanse, I knew that we were moving on, forging ahead. I knew that beyond the horizon lay answers to my most important questions. I knew, that as day changed into night and night overtook the day, that time was the

[11] A lantern carried at the stern of a ship to serve as a signal at night.

one thing that I could count on. I had a sure knowing that with each day, each hour and each minute that passed, there was a destination that I was working toward. I knew that by working hard to keep *The Pharaoh* safe, I would get to the end of this journey - to see my father.

10

The storm that came upon us on the fifty-seventh day was sudden and brutal. We had just sailed past the first group of tiny Windward Islands of Martinique, Barbados and St. Lucia, in the Caribbean Sea and our first destination was close. My brothers came out like a band of marching triplets to see the islands. They had been inside their cabins so long, they looked pale and pasty. Their paunches were a lot larger than when we left Quitta. There was an abundance of good food from the cook's kitchen, and a seemingly endless stream of expensive drinks and cigars. It was evident that my brothers over-indulged in everything.

"Good morning!" said Harald looking me up and down.

I had my shirt off, and my hair was in a ponytail. My muscles were rippling, and sweat poured off my back as I carried the ropes and sails I had mended.

"Good morning, Harald," I answered.

"Good morning," the other two chorused.

I nodded to the two, "Good Morning."

"You have been busy," Harald said with a smile that didn't quite reach his eyes.

"Just a little," I said with a smile that didn't quite reach my eyes.

"Do you need help with anything?" I asked.

I walked unhurriedly to another part of the deck. I could feel their eyes boring holes in my back. I tuned them out.

Suddenly, a tumultuous roll of thunder roared in my ears. It was so unexpected; it startled me badly, and I dropped the sails I was carrying. I turned to face the direction of the thunder and there, in the south-east were huge ominous black clouds that seemed to be clashing and overshadowing each other. Lightning zigzagged its way through the clouds, darkening, deepening, changing shape, and expanding in every direction.

The wind suddenly changed direction. The weather cooled abruptly. Then, there was an unexpected stillness.... Out of the blue, Captain Laarsen began to shout orders. The deck became a hive of activity. My brothers were nowhere to be seen. They silently disappeared somewhere into the bowels of the ship.

"This is going to be a hurricane!" Johan exclaimed, "And it's coming straight at us!"

"It will hit us starboard!"

"All hands on deck!"

The forecastle emptied, and every sailor was on deck securing ropes, tying things down and helping in any way they could. Twilight came upon us rudely as the clouds seemed to broil and roil blackly. The clouds seemed to influence the ocean to imitate its actions. It was as though the heavens and the oceans were in a deadly wrestling match.

The storm, when it came, was ferocious and brutal. It lifted us high on the waves and cruelly let us go into free fall as we sailed right into its fiery eye. We had to sail right into the eye of the storm because it was the only way we could prevent being slammed sideways and tipped over, ship, contents and all, into the rabid ocean.

The rain pounded at us relentlessly, and winds from hades came at us from every corner. Together, the water and the wind colluded frantically and threatened to break the ship apart and pull us under. The waves got really high and splashed over the deck. We clung to anything we could find for dear life. Suddenly, a line broke, and the mainsail flapped around violently threatening to break the main mast. Captain Larsen shouted more orders. In response, Johan shouted his orders and men ran across the deck. A sailor I had seen around but didn't know very well, ran up to the mast. He had his dangerous looking rigging knife in his hand, and he expertly climbed the eighty-foot mast. He clung to the mast and cut the rigging lines. His swift action saved the mast and the ship. Just as the sailor climbed back down, another forceful wind blew, and the ship bucked wildly. About three feet of water gushed onto the deck. The man lost his balance and slipped into the water. He dropped his knife and tried to clutch wildly at anything. In the end, he just clutched at the water. The treacherous water yanked him away and maliciously tipped him over the edge of the ship. We watched in horror as he flailed and screamed. His screams were truncated as the icy cold water took his breath away. We listened in vain for sounds of life. All we heard were the terrible sounds of howling winds, angry waves and the sounds of terror pounding in our hearts. The sailor saved the ship but lost his life.

Captain Laarsen was masterful in the way he handled *The Pharaoh*. The guests huddled in the captain's cabin, eyes wide open and tried hard not to be afraid of the reckless heaving movements. I now understood why my father hired Laarsen, Johan and the crew. They were simply the best! Like everything Papi did, he always required perfection. Johan and the crew, including me of course, were perfect or close to perfect when it came to maneuvering the ship through rough waves.

It was a miracle when the storm finally broke. Johan and most of the sailors were wounded while fighting the storm. They had slashed arms and legs. Some had cuts to their faces and heads. The ship's doctor had to stitch up Johan's leg which was cut by a piece of mast. He and the other sailors were plied with whiskey to help them bear their pain and suffering. As a result, we were shorthanded on the watches, and I offered to do double duty.

As if by some tacit consent, my brothers and I climbed down the companionways that led into the holds, and deep into the bowels of the ship. They opened each hold, and we inspected everything. Not only did we need to make sure that all the investments were secure, but we also needed to make sure that there were no leaks anywhere that could sink the ship. We, the four brothers, stood on each side of the ship for our "look out duties." My brothers stayed for one four-hour watch.

Because we were so shorthanded, I climbed up the rigging and pulled down the torn sails. I sat with the sailmaker, and we mended the sails with the sailmaker's palm and needle. The sailmaker taught me to use the sailmaker's palm like a thimble to help push the needle through the thick layers of canvas. Then we climbed the rigging again and put all the sails in place. After being battered by the wind and the waves, the ship needed attention, and I got out a large paint brush to paint the exposed wood so that it wouldn't rot.

Once again, the ocean mirrored the sky when evening came. It was calm and inviting and the night was cool and soft. All evidence of the brouhaha of the weather was erased. After almost eighteen hours of work that day, I was exhausted. I had just finished the last watch at the bow of the ship. My legs refused to lead me to my cabin. The cabins were damp anyway, and I didn't cherish the thought of sleeping on a damp mattress in the musky air. My feet wouldn't move; they felt like I was wearing lead shoes. My body was beaten and my eyes bleary as I made out the ship's boat nearby. I uncovered the tarpaulin that covered it, fell inside the boat, pulled the tarpaulin over my head and promptly fell asleep.

PART 2

"For everything there is a season,

and a time for every matter

under heaven:

a time to be born, and a time to die"

King Solomon

11

Kø opened his eyes by degrees. He would have opened them instantly if he could have, but his eyes, like the rest of his body, were reluctant to do his bidding. His body felt like a felled tree-trunk that had been left behind.

The first thing he felt was the periodic breeze that attempted to cool his still feverish flesh. He could hear the slight swishing sound of a curtain lifted by the breeze. He could hear other sounds he couldn't identify. The sounds were garbled high-pitched nonsense like cawing crows fighting over leftover carcasses. Low dissonant sounds continued to disturb his peace. The sounds made him want to open his eyes wider, but the glue that held his eyelids together were thick, gummy and stubborn.

Kø fell into a slumber again. His dreams were terrifying. They were filled with eyes. Blue eyes that hated him, eyes that laughingly hypnotized him into a boat. He dreamed of blue-eyed girls with dimples feeding him with a highly alcoholic mixture of *pito and* palm wine. The eyes accused him of being late. For his punishment, the eyes attempted to drown him in the Quitta lagoon. Kø struggled to wake up. He tried again and again. Finally, after several desperate attempts, his eyes obeyed him.

There were no words to describe the color of the tattered curtain that shielded the window when Kø's eyes finally opened. He couldn't decide whether what he was seeing was real thing or whether it was his imagination. Whatever color the curtain used to be, it was no longer that color. Sun, soap, water and time had eaten up the original color. The curtain playfully fluttered and welcomed the breeze, totally oblivious to its pitiful state.

Beyond the curtain, the day was slowly dying, and dusk was taking over, painting the sky with crazy indecisive colors. It should have been a peaceful time, but some women quarreled incessantly not too far away. Kø couldn't follow what they were saying because of their strange accent. He just wished they would shut up long enough for him to control his violent headache.

As the breeze played with the curtain, it lifted it high enough so Kø could see the tops of the palm trees in the distance. He could also see the rusty zinc roofs of shanties. It was familiar, yet so unfamiliar. The smell of the sea was familiar, as was the acrid smell of stagnant water. He would later discover, that the smells he couldn't identify, were the smells of cane being boiled into sugar and molasses and also distilled into rum.

A violent movement to his left caused him to turn his head suddenly. Loose cannons clashed in his head as he came face to face with coarse brown fabric in front of something that felt like hard card. The fabric served as a curtain that obviously divided the room. Beyond the curtain were sounds of a woman thrashing about in the throes of an intense orgasm. The deep grunts that the man emitted, and the violent movement of the bed beyond indicated that the man was desperate to reach and fall off a deliciously perilous precipice in tandem with his partner. "*Mawu Ga!*" Kø thought to himself in deep consternation, "Oh, my Great God!"

"Dear God! Where am I? What place is this? Who are these people? What is going on?" he wondered.

"Oh, Lass!" the man beyond the curtain growled contentedly. He had successfully and blissfully fallen over the precipice just as he had anticipated. "*Lang may yer lum reek!*[12] You're simply t' bes'!" he said gently.

He gently disengaged himself from her, blew through his lips and made himself comfortable in the middle of the bed.

She giggled like a little girl. She spoke in an unusual *Creolsk* language which Kø couldn't quite understand. It sounded like a mixture of English, Danish and something else.

"Tenk yu, P.G! Man, yu not easy at ahll!!"

Her voice was young and girlish. She sounded like a choirmaster's favorite soprano soloist. She and her man were both totally oblivious to the trauma they had caused the man who had just woken up after a two-week coma. She turned to the bedside table and poured out a generous amount of rum. She handed it to Peegee who beamed his appreciation. She carefully poured a small quantity into her own glass. It was her "keeping him company" drink. She hated getting drunk. There was nothing she hated more than not being in control. But her companion's mood turned ugly whenever she refused to drink with him, so she learned that saying a simple "yes, sir" or "yes, dear" made life so much easier... and definitely more profitable.

---

[12] Scottish for "May you live long and prosper!"

Peegee threw back his rum and swallowed it in one large gulp. He handed her the glass, and she filled it again and got out of bed. She proceeded to dress in short quick movements and by the time Peegee emptied his second glass, she was fully dressed.

"Mi 'av tings fi luk 'bout Peegee." She sounded businesslike. The girlishness was all gone.

"I 'av fi go luk 'bout di sea man an' mek 'im drink more medicine. Me 'av many tings fi luk 'bout..." she said again.

Peegee settled deeper into her bed. They both knew what her "errands" consisted of. Invariably, she would, during her so-called "errands," look for a man in the many drinking taverns in Coral Bay, who would quickly empty his pockets for her exceptional services.

"*Yer aff yer heid!* T' man from t' sea will surely die soon, Lassie," he said huffily. "Ye mark my words!"

"Today, Daffodil, you will be mine and mine alone!"

Plundering loot was in Peegee's blood. He had left the cold, boring village on the banks of Loch Lomond in Scotland and found his way to the sunny Caribbean where he found his true vocation. Peegee lived for the adrenalin rush of piracy. He loved the danger, the excitement, and the immense reward. Peegee's name was known all the way from the Danish Virgin Islands to Brazil. To many sailors, he was a man to be feared.

Legend had it, that during an intense struggle for a Portuguese ship, Peegee was shot just below his left clavicle, injuring his left arm. Being an ambidextrous man, he continued to fight with the uninjured hand until he defeated the owners and killed the captain. Then, he dug his dagger into his shoulder and gouged out the bullet. He took one look at it and fell into a dead faint. After the wound healed, he hung the offensive bullet on a chain which he decided to wear around his neck every day. It nestled among the curly red hairs of his chest where it hung like a menacing African talisman. It was then that he earned the nickname *Geepeegee,* Great Pirate Gerald or Peegee for short.

Peegee tossed back another large mouthful of rum, stroked his fiery red beard and leisurely studied his companion from head to toe and back again. She was lovely, indeed delectable. Petite and svelte, she had a heart-shaped face that ended in a small pointy chin. Her curly, long, black, waist length hair framed her face. Her eyes, an interesting greenish-brown color, slanted upwards at the outer corner, indicating an Asian ancestor somewhere in her lineage. They were framed by incredibly thick, long, black lashes that looked like she had kohl permanently outline her eyes. When she fixed her eyes on a man she wanted, it was as though she had pinned him to a wall. And the man was permanently "pinned" until she got what she wanted from him.

She was an exotic mix of Asian, African and Portuguese and she made Peegee's blood rage. She met him passion for passion, and she was the only woman who satisfied his every fantasy and assuaged his infinite lust.

He licked his lips lustfully as he beheld her fine figure. He mentally measured her vital statistics. He remembered her breasts, soft and malleable under his large hairy hands. Her waist was so small; he needed just one hand to span the small of her back. And ah, her bottom was just what he needed. It was round and pert and enough to cushion them both when he dug deep into the wet sweetness of her secret place. He couldn't have enough of her - just like he couldn't have enough of pirating ships. And today, he had no intention of letting her go. For the right price, she would do his every bidding. Today, Peegee intended to have her till he was sated and deliciously, deliriously, drained!

"Daffodil," said Peegee gently, "Lass, 'an' me my coat will ye?"

He dug into the recesses of the pocket of the coat she handed him and brought out a fistful of gold nuggets in his pudgy fingers.

"See this, my dear?" The gold nuggets glinted dully in the darkened room, and he grinned at her astonishment.

She couldn't take her eyes off the precious metal.

"These are for ye…." He opened his fist and gave her an eyeful.

"For me?" she squealed. Delight spread all over her face.

"Yes. For ye, if ye'll spend t' rest o' t' night wiv me."

Before she could answer, he added:

"An' Daffodil," he said gently. "keep in min' lass, there's more where this came from!"

"Of course, I will, Peegee!" she wrapped her arms around him giggling like a schoolgirl who had just won a prize for best student.

"Of course, I will!" she squealed thinking about her good fortune. "Your wish is my command!"

She held out both her hands and chuckling, he released the precious metal. She wrapped the glinting pieces carefully in her kerchief. Later, after Peegee left, she would hide it in an old battered chamber pot under her bed. No one would ever think of robbing the contents of an old chipped grimy chamber pot! She grinned delightedly. She was much closer to her dream now. She would give the good pirate whatever he wanted, and she would get whatever she wanted.

Daffodil stripped off her clothing one by one, giving him an eyeful of her assets. She looked at him provocatively and moistened her lips with her little pink tongue. The Captain tossed back another helping of rum. He groaned when she turned around and did a little dance for him, and he leaped off the bed to join his Lady Torment. Considering his considerable bulk, he was extremely agile.

"Turn 'round, Lass," Captain growled, "'old onto that table."

He impatiently turned her around himself, and she gripped the table near the wall. He positioned his huge erection near the parting of her buttocks. He pushed, and she squealed.

"Come 'ere, Lass," he grabbed her waist and pulled her closer. He whispered into her ear.

"Gimme it, baby!" He molded her breasts and teased her nipples.

Sounds of pure lust filled the room.

Divided by just a rough burlap curtain, Kø covered his eyes with his pillow. It was as though in covering his eyes he could blot out the sounds and accompanying images of what was happening just a few inches away. Daffodil groaned loudly. Kø stuffed his fist in his mouth. His sudden erection was painful and unrelenting, splitting him down the middle. He was an unwilling participant in the happenings just a spit away. He hadn't eaten for weeks, and his body was still weak from his recent ordeal. His mind was hazy, and his soul was aching from the treachery of those people on the ship, the apparent abandonment of his father, the boiling anger of a jealous lover and a young woman who got him in all this trouble. And yet, his sex was alive and vibrant and throbbing. It callously and painfully hauled him, body and soul, into the immediate present. Passion gripped him and would not let him go. His discombobulation was complete.

Just then, Daffodil screamed as the throes of her orgasm began to grip her, the pirate rudely withdrew, leaving her whimpering and wanting. He laid her on the table and stood between her legs. He spread her legs wide and put her feet on his shoulders. Grunting, Peegee pounded away till Daffodil thought she would split in two. When the Captain sensed her shaking again, he separated himself from her and carried her to her bed. She was almost in tears with wanting, but Peegee sat on the edge of the bed and waited till she cooled off. Then he spread her wide again and with force impaled her once again. Daffodil wrapped her arms tightly around his neck, and wrapped her legs around his waist; she imprisoned him in a vice he was happy to be in. He gave, and she took, she gave, and he took and together the earth moved and moved again.

Kø's bed moved in tandem with the force of their movements. He stuffed his pillow in his mouth and swallowed his groans. One hand gripped his manhood hard. Sweat dripped from his brow and his body. His mind was emptied of every thought. Daffodil's cries increased. The pirate's breath quickened. Kø's unwilling excitement escalated. Daffodil screamed as her orgasm erupted. It took her over the edge, and she felt as though it came in waves: wave after wave after wave of bliss. The Captain let out a slow, low growl as he emptied his copious seed into her. Kø tightened his hands around himself and released his seed also. Stars went off in his head and the tears that leaked from the corners of his eyes chased one another and soaked the pillow. He was disgusted and relieved, confused, clear-headed and satiated at the same time.

"Where am I?" he thought, putting the pillow aside.

"Who are these people?" The word 'people' had as much disgust as he could muster.

"How did I get here?" he wondered.

"Where on earth am I?"

"What will become of me?"

A few feet away, deep, contented snores mingled with lighter, satisfied sounds of slumber.

Kø lay in the wet bed. Weakness gripped him violently like an angry dog trying to separate flesh from bone. The bed was soaked with tears, sweat, and other bodily emissions. His stomach rumbled with hunger. His misery was complete. He lay in it for what felt like hours. In the distance, a cock crowed, and another one answered. The breeze had stilled, but it was cool, and the stillness somehow calmed his chaotic thoughts.

"With the cock crowing," he thought to himself wearily, "it means it's about three in the morning."

It was no different from the sounds from back home in Quitta. He hadn't been able to sleep after the 'episode,' and he wondered what he should do. He felt trapped. Trapped by jealous men and flighty women, trapped by angry brothers who couldn't accept that the same blood that flowed through them flowed through him, so much so, that they wanted him buried in a watery grave and now he was trapped in a strange land, in a shanty by a wanton woman and her pugnacious lover.

Wearily, Kø got out of bed. The night was quiet, and the secrets of the day seemed to be securely locked away by the darkness. He made his way to the window to see what lay beyond the nondescript curtain. There just might be a way of escape. A floorboard creaked noisily as he stepped on it. He jumped sideways and crashed into a small table laden with tin containers and bottles of assorted medicines. Kø instinctively flattened himself against the wall; his chest heaved with fear. At the disturbance, Peegee leaped out of bed and in one fluid movement, grabbed his guns and raced toward the sound entirely forgetting his state of undress. Kø found himself staring down the barrel of one lethal looking gun then the other. He finally looked at the owner of the guns and wasn't sure which was more fearful… the huge naked redhead with fiery green eyes in front of him or the lethal looking pistols thrust in his face. Peegee had a long unruly red beard that merged halfway with the curly red hair on his chest. His hair stood on end. Kø willed his eyes not to move downwards, but they seemed to have a will of their own. With shock at the sheer size of the man's member, Kø decided it would be safer to look into the gentleman's eyes with his hands up in the air. Maybe, just maybe, he might find mercy there. They were about the same height, but the man was more than twice his size.

"He awake!" a female voice cried. "Di sea man finally 'wake!"

The relief Kø felt at the sound of her voice was like torrential rain after a drought.

"Aye! Aye! I see tha'!" growled the giant lowering his guns and taking a sheet from his lover's hands to cover his nakedness.

"Gave us a scare, ye did!" he added looking Kø over.

Daffodil hovered around Kø like a mother hen touching his arms, his back, and his chest and trying to determine whether he was all right.

"D'ye speak English, man? Or Danish?" Peegee asked Kø.

"I speak both," he answered slowly.

Eyebrows of both spectators were raised considerably.

"Where are you from?"

"Quitta," he answered, "on the Guinea Coast of Africa."

100

Both jaws dropped, and eyebrows disappeared into both hairlines.

Kø looked from one comical face to the other and relaxed. Perchance, they were not as dangerous as he imagined.

"And wha's your name? Peegee asked.

"My name is Hans Kondo Quist," he answered, weariness washed over his body, and his voice was strained.

He looked a little past Daffodil and addressed the wall. With the memories of what just happened still fresh in his mind, he couldn't bear to look at her.

"Can I have some food to eat please, Ma'am? I'm starving."

Kø chewed on the jerk chicken and breadfruit slowly. The jerk chicken was spicy and tasty, the breadfruit cold and bland. He ate it anyway knowing that he needed to regain his strength. He washed down the food with a little rum, sputtered a bit but kept on eating.

When his hosts were fully dressed, they sat across from him and observed him. Peegee sat on his haunches with his fingers loosely crossed between his knees. Occasionally, he stroked his mustache and gathered his beard to a fine point. His ruddy face was inscrutable, but inevitably he always went back to a default position: ankles crossed, and fingers laced loosely between his knees. He set his guns on a table within arm's reach and waited.

If he didn't know better, Kø would have sworn, looking at her face, that Daffodil was someone's baby sister. But when she fixed her gaze on him, he was torn between the need to run and hide because of the tremendous sexual energy that emanated from her, and the need to protect her from the big bad world.

Her round black eyes were the eyes of timelessness. Eyes that had seen too much too early. Eyes that once had hope. It wasn't as though she had no hope; she just came to accept that her lot in life was for the pleasure of men. She was no fool though. Men loved her body for pleasure, and she loved the gold and silver coins they paid her for her services. She plied them with rum and so her clients, mostly pirates, sailors and some men of substance, were too inebriated to notice, and too careless with their ill-gotten fortune to care that they had overpaid her. It worked out well for both pirate and prostitute. Besides, she had a plan to escape this life. It was a plan she had been crafting out for some time. She was patiently waiting for the right opportunity to present itself.

Kø looked around the place. The room was a basic square room built with wood. It was sparsely furnished, and the main furniture was the bed which was made of strong and sturdy dark wood. To his practiced carpenter's eye, Kø saw that it was well made and could well withstand the demands of her trade. There was a sofa, a chair and a table in one corner. The table was laden with kitchen utensils and food. Another table was pushed near a window. It had nothing on it. Everything, surprisingly, was neatly arranged. There was only one door through which one could come and go. A flutter of her hand drew Kø's attention back to Daffodil:

"How did you get here, Kø?" Daffodil asked.

She went about in her quick way. She fetched Peegee another glass and served him some more rum. Kø was amazed at her composure. He was still reluctant to meet her eyes because he was still embarrassed by her, or rather, he was embarrassed by *their* recent escapade. Instead, he looked at the Pirate. Pirate Gerald met his eyes trying to read him.

"Where am I?" Kø asked.

"You're on the Island of St. John," answered Peegee.

"This place is called Salt Pond Bay!" Daffodil interjected.

"How did you get here, Kø?" she continued, "You have been in a coma for almost two weeks."

The fork Kø was holding clattered noisily onto the plate.

"May I please have a bath?" he asked losing appetite suddenly.

Peegee and Daffodil looked at each other. Silently, Daffodil took him to an outside bathroom that stood on its own. It was made of old tin sheets on four sides, and there was a metal bolt to offer one privacy, but there was no roof over it. The elements were given free rein to be voyeurs as one performed one's daily ablutions from an old tin bucket filled with water from a well. Floating helplessly on the water was an old pail that had been used for different things. At this stage of the pail's sorry, haphazard life, its duty was to pour water on people who needed a bucket bath.

Kø scrubbed the grime, salt, and sand from his body. His tears mingled with well water as he rinsed himself off. He began to think about his plight and those he had left behind. Thinking made him dizzy, the walls of the bathroom began to spin and close in on him. He tried desperately to get out. He thought he pulled the bolt... But he wasn't sure... Because all he felt was a floating sensation. Mercifully, the day turned into black.

It was another fourteen hours before Kø awoke again. This time, he opened his eyes suddenly to some smoke infiltrating his lungs. There, in front of his nose, burning something that smelled like incense and dead leaves, was Daffodil looking as beautiful as ever.

"You're back!" she said cheerfully, setting the ugly, beat up tin with its smoking contents, down on the small table beside his bed. "Don't worry; you just need your strength back. Take it easy now."

"We didn't expect you to survive at all!" She paused and fed him a dark bitter concoction. It tasted like the boiled neem tree leaves his mother used to prepare for him anytime he was ill. He grimaced. She followed it with a sweeter drink made with ginger, lemongrass, and molasses. He drank thirstily and asked for more. His throat was so parched. She covered him with a thin sheet and tucked it all around him. Then she straightened the already straightened bottles of concoctions on the table. When she finally sat down on a wooden armchair close to his bed, she arranged the tiny pleats of her dress, so they fell in perfect order.

"When they realized you weren't dead, they brought you here, so I could help you. You see, my mother used to heal people. She knew a lot about herbs and potions. She passed the knowledge on to me."

"Is your mother here?" Kø asked.

"She died eight years ago. I learned to take care of myself from then on."

"What about your father?" Kø persisted.

"I never knew him." Her voice was devoid of emotion, and something told Kø not to pursue the matter. Kø changed the subject.

"Your name seems funny to me... why are you called Daffodil? Isn't that a flower or something?" he asked.

Daffodil smiled. "People always ask me that question. I was born the year wild daffodils bloomed on the island."

"There was a terrible hurricane that year," she continued, "and everything was destroyed. People lost hope because they lost everything. They really suffered because they had no food or water. The hurricane destroyed many farms. One day, they woke up, and wild daffodils had bloomed everywhere. It hadn't happened before and hasn't happened again since then. To my mother, Daffodil meant hope.

"Your name also seems funny to me..." she said suddenly turning to him.

"Why are you called Kø?"

Kø ignored the question.

"How did you find me?" he asked her.

"Why are you evading the question?"

"I'm not evading your question..."

"You are..."

"There are things I want to know."

"Don't you think I want to know some things as well?" she insisted.

"I will tell you everything, but please tell me how I was found."

Kø pulled up a chair and sat opposite Daffodil. His thumbs tapped at each other, circled around each other and tapped again over and over again – pap pap papapap.....

"Two young boys found you at the beach not far from here," she said, pointing to a clearing beyond the curtain he couldn't see.

"They told us later that they went out looking for crabs when they saw something lying in the sand. They came running out of the fog as though they had seen *duppy*.[13] They were terrified, and so when they pointed frantically to the direction of the sea, some men went running to the bay......"

"What did they see?" Kø asked curiously leaning forward in his chair. "Tell me what made them so afraid? Who were the two boys? Was I in the water or was I on the land?"

"Do you want to hear the story or not?" answered Daffodil pertly. She crossed her arms across her chest.

"Of course, I do…"

"Then stop interrupting me!"

Kø sat back looking at her in slight disgust. She was like a bossy little sister.

---

[13] Ghost

"Well?" she asked, waiting....

"Well what?" he asked impatiently.

"Well, will you stop interrupting me and let me tell the story?" she retorted.

Kø wanted to ram his hand down her throat and get the story out. She decided to clamp her mouth shut till he showed some respect. Fortunately, they were both saved from a full-blown argument by some commotion at the door.

Two men stood at the door. One of the men, tall, gaunt and lanky, nicknamed Hololegs stood there. Hololegs' trousers were several inches too short, and they showed off his hairy ankles. He secured the waist of his trousers tightly with a piece of leftover string. He had a mournful, longsuffering look, as though he had been denied of nourishment for a long time. No-one remembered what Hololegs' real name was. It wasn't as though he didn't eat enough. In fact, Hololegs was a voracious eater. It was just that no matter what he ate, he just couldn't put on weight. He was nicknamed Hololegs because his friends said all the food he ate must go somewhere and they concluded that the food settled right there somewhere inside his thin, long, hollow legs.

His best friend, Boussy, stood there beside him. His arms were akimbo, and his bow legs stood solidly on the ground like a man about to take part in a wrestling match. His shirt threatened to tear apart with every movement of his broad chest, thick arms and thick neck. He wore loose knee-length shorts to accommodate his bulging thigh muscles.

"Anybody 'ome?" Boussy boomed in his loud commanding voice.

"Come in Boussy, come in Hololegs," Daffodil said opening the door wider.

Ever since they deposited Kø there, they came to check on him every day. And yet, every time they came to Daffodil's home, they would stand at the door, shuffling their feet, reluctant to enter in.

"He's awake!" said Daffodil delightedly ignoring their reticence. "The man from the sea is awake now!"

Eager to see their 'patient,' they temporarily forgot their discomfort and pushed their way into the room. Kø was attempting to stand up when they entered, but dizziness washed over him, and he fell back onto the bed, still weak from his recent ordeal. He looked from one man to the other and recognized no-one, but he felt an affinity to both in a way he couldn't understand.

"This is Boussy, Kø," said Daffodil. "Boussy carried you in when you were found."

The men couldn't stop grinning as they nodded to both Kø and Daffodil. "Mi ketch me 'fraid!'" barked Boussy. "You scared us when we found you!"

"We cuda swear seh u ded!" Interjected Hololegs. "We were certain you would die!"

"Tenk Gawd Lisa u awrite naw!" said Boussy smiling. "But we thank God *Lisa* you're better now."

With herculean effort, Kø stood up and embraced each of his benefactors.

"I owe all three of you my life! May the gods of my ancestors and the Almighty God favor you and reward you for saving my life."

"Almighty God, Lisa, was with you else you wouldn't have lived; we can tell you that for sure!" Boussy exclaimed.

"I'm so glad you're both here!" Kø said. His eyes held a slightly mischievous look as he glanced at Daffodil.

"Daffodil was just telling me how you found me. But you can relay the story much better than she can, I'm sure."

Daffodil made a face at him and laughed good-naturedly.

12

Boussy settled himself comfortably in the seat given him, and took on an air of self-importance. His voice was deep, commanding and brooked no nonsense and no unnecessary interruption. The veins in his thick neck stood out like an angry weapon.

"Ok, Daffodil," he said, "set down! Lemme tell di stowrie."

Daffodil sat, and Hololegs lounged by the window. He moved his half-moon shaped head from person to person and observed everything with mournful interest.

"Alla we did a eat brukfurst kina laite in de monin', sake of de fog," Boussy began.

"Most people were enjoying a late breakfast on the day you were found, because of the eerie fog."

"Di fishaman dem never cuda goa sea. An, nuffa we whe 'af grounds was na' able go fi work 'pon fi we grounds," He continued.

111

*"The fishermen couldn't go out to sea, and those of us who farmed
the land couldn't find our way to the farm."*

"I was preparing to do some blacksmithing jobs at my good
neighbor, Hololegs' home when we heard the commotion,"
Boussy said nodding at Hololegs. Boussy's voice took on an
imitation of a whisper.

"It was a strange, eerie morning and not many people were
about because visibility was so poor. Even in their homes, people
spoke in hushed tones. The fog was thick, grey and heavy and it
covered the whole island. No-one had ever seen such a heavy
fog ever before. It was past mid-day when the fog began to
slowly separate itself from the land. It peeled itself off from the
sea, the land and the trees like a snake sloughing off its skin.

Two terrified boys came running out of the fog as though some
Jonkonnu[14] was chasing them! We were all so alarmed, that about
six or seven of us hurriedly grabbed an array of weapons and
headed for the beach. I ran all the way to the Salt Pond Beach in
the direction the boys pointed. I tried asking them to describe
exactly what they saw, but they were either too fearful to
answer or too out of breath from all the running. We saw
something lying in the sand when we got to the beach but

---

[14] No-one knows for sure where the name *Jonkonnu* comes from. Some say it refers to an
eighteenth century West African King John Canoe. Others believe it represents a sloppy English
pronunciation of a French phrase 'gens inconnu', meaning unknown or masked people.

couldn't identify what it was. All we knew was that something lay lifeless in the sand. The boys stood a few feet behind us, and you could see sheer terror in their eyes! They clutched each other for support, ready to flee for dear life if the thing moved. I now understood why they couldn't describe what it was they saw. The sight was indescribable!"

Kø looked at him in wonderment, wondering what they really saw. He reckoned that they would tell him in due course and he decided to wait.

Boussy continued. His voice was still a semi-whisper.

"The fog still covered part of the thing, and we just couldn't decipher what it was. The seven of us moved closer in unison and formed a semi-circle ready to attack or flee if the thing moved."

"Finally, after several minutes, I made it out!"

Boussy shut his eyes in recollection at the weird apparition in the sand. Hololegs shook his head at the memory.

"Lying face down in the sand was the head of a man. His long brown hair was splayed on the sand like a lost fan. His body was still covered by fog, and they couldn't decide whether his head was decapitated or not. Beside the man's head was the head of a dolphin. We stood there aghast and unable to comprehend the sight before us!"

"A dolphin?" said Kø, amazed.

113

"A dolphin!" emphasized Boussy.

"What we don't understand is how a dolphin rescued you," said Daffodil. "We think it gave its life for you. It died so you could live."

"I used to swim with Dolphins," Kø said slowly.

"There was one I used to play with all the time. I knew she followed the ship when we left the Guinea Coast! I had no idea she followed us from the Atlantic Ocean to the Caribbean Sea."

"Mercifully," continued Boussy, impatient to finish his story, "the sun braved its way through the clouds and the fog began to lift some more. As the fog lifted, we inched closer, walking almost shoulder to shoulder."

For the first time, Hololegs interjected.

"A few brave women walked several steps behind us, arms around each other. My wife was one of them!"

"The fog finally lifted enough for us to see that indeed it was the body of a man and that man was you, Kø!" said Boussy, his voice came back to normal.

Boussy and Hololegs were quiet as they reminisced once again about the events of that day.

Shielding Kø's body protectively was the dolphin. Its nose was just above Kø's head and its tail fin curled around his feet, preventing the waves from doing any more damage to his legs or washing him back into the sea.

Boussy continued. His voice became much softer than it had ever been.

"Finally, I broke away from the band of people who were just staring at the unbelievable sight. I bent down and pushed you onto your back. Your long hair had covered your face, and I felt your neck to see if I could feel your pulse. Water ran in steady rivulets down the side of your mouth. The pulse was faint, but thank God, you were still alive! I shouted to anyone who could hear to bring us blankets! We needed blankets to keep you warm. No-one had blankets."

"My wife was there," interjected Hololegs again. "She quickly came forward, took the turban off her head and shook it out with one vigorous shake. She covered you from your neck to your knees. The flesh on your feet and toes were all wrinkled and peeling because you had stayed in the water too long. Boussy hauled you over one shoulder as though you were a rag doll and brought you here. If anyone could save you, we knew Daffodil could."

Boussy and Hololegs looked at each other, trying to find meaning to what had happened. They remembered how everyone quietly left the beach, each battling with their own thoughts at the incredulity of what they had just seen. They decided, that Kø was certainly a man on a mission. Some things, they concluded silently, defied explanation.

Kø was lost in thought. He remembered the prayers of his uncle, the King of Quitta, the Fetish priest and the Lutheran priest. He remembered the prayers of his mother and his beloved fiancée, Eva. Someone's prayers were definitely answered. That's all he knew. He was thankful to all who prayed for him and even more grateful to those who rescued him, and he said so with feeling.

Boussy and Hololegs didn't stay much longer after that. They promised to come the following day to talk some more. Kø lay spent long after they left. He shut his eyes and thought about the meaning of his life. Nothing made sense.

Daffodil cooked Kø some goat head broth, which she said would help build up his strength. The broth, which Daffodil called "mannish water," was liberally laced with rum. After several helpings, Kø's mind stopped wandering in circles. The questions that chased themselves in his mind were blotted out. Slightly drunk, sleep snatched him up and took him to a place of peace.

From then on, Kø always woke up to the acrid smell of smoke as Daffodil burned feathers, dried roots and incense while she chanted ancient verses over him. He woke to the putrid, nauseating smells of herbal concoctions which she force-fed him. She had small hands, but they were extremely dexterous, determined and resilient. If her mother had been alive, she would have been proud that her daughter had embraced everything she had taught her. Daffodil pushed the thought of her mother out of her mind and went about her business.

What needed to be done, needed to be done.

13

It became evident that Daffodil needed space to conduct her 'business.' Sometimes, her 'business' took place in the most unexpected places, in an inn on the island, in a dark alley or an empty canoe when there was no time for long dalliances, and at other times, it was conducted on the large bed in her home. It was clear that since there was only one bedroom in the house that Kø was in the way of her earning a living. So by tacit consent, Kø prepared to take his nightly walk just before Daffodil took her nightly walk. They walked on parallel paths but in opposite directions. He always walked down the lonely path to the shore; to the spot where he was found. His shoulders dejected, his head bowed at the impossibility of his situation. Daffodil, on the other hand, with her head held high, walked into the crowds and often found her way to select groups of wealthy men. At other times, she chose to go to the shore at Coral Bay where the Captains of ships as well as sailors were looking for some fun with a lady of the night.

Daffodil chose to visit the Inn and Out Tavern for the evening. She painted her voluptuous lips a deep red, curved her lips into a sensuous smile as walked into the crowd wearing a pretty gown. She blended in as though she belonged there. She scanned the room slowly, taking her time to assess each man in the room. She pulled down the front of her dress slightly and exposed more bosom. The man that met her approval was young, athletic and well-dressed. He looked slightly familiar, but she decided he must look like an old customer. She surmised by his timepiece, rings, and hessian boots that he was certainly wealthy. His eyes scanned the room as he stroked his mustache and short beard. He had a calculating look she recognized. On his left hand, he wore a wedding ring, and he had an expensive signet ring on the ring finger of his right hand. The ring had some sort of a crest on it. She couldn't make it out, but that didn't matter. She moved closer to him but made sure she was out of his line of vision. When she observed the slight bulge in his trousers, she took short, determined steps straight to him. With her girlish laugh, she bent over him exposing the tops of her breasts and said in her low girlish voice:

"Would a gentleman buy a thirsty lady a drink?"

When he got over his initial surprise, his sky-blue eyes lit up as he surveyed the exquisite sight before him. He looked her over from her bosom to the outline of her hips and back to her lush, black, waist-length hair, aquiline nose, and full voluptuous lips. When he looked into her eyes, a slight movement of his body toward her, told her she had a done deal. She sat down in one fluid movement before he answered in the affirmative.

"I will buy you a drink, of course!" smiled the man. "What will you have?"

"What do you want me to have?" Daffodil asked coyly. "Choose something for me."

Before long, Daffodil and Mark had settled in an animated conversation, and Mark felt he had known her for ages. Drink loosened his tongue and released his inhibitions. The more Daffodil looked at him, the more he drowned in the seductive pool of her eyes. It wasn't long before Mark asked Daffodil to go for a ride with him in his carriage. By the time they got to his plantation, Daffodil's gown was around her waist, and his trousers were around his ankles. She was bouncing in his lap as the carriage rocked over the cobbled stones.

As they drove in, Daffodil broke from his passionate embrace long enough to notice a crest on the post of the gate. The crest at the entrance of the plantation looked very familiar...so did the stone walls and the huge windmill. She had a strange feeling of déjà vu…

"Are you ok?" asked Mark, concerned.

"I'm quite all right," she answered, straightening her clothes.

"Just a little hot." She fanned herself and gave her childlike giggle. As Daffodil stepped out of the carriage, it all came back to her. She remembered every detail of the Plantation. She knew every nook and cranny of the place. And she knew exactly who Mark was now. Her stomach was tied in knots, but she kept her thoughts to herself and her emotions tightly reigned in.

Meanwhile, as Kø walked down toward the beaten path to the cove, the full moon gave as much light as it could, but its light was somber and temporal. The tangled, creeping undergrowth gave off a rich verdant smell as Kø trudged onward. The breeze swayed the trunks of trees and lifted their leaves. Leaves of every size, shape, and length stretched out toward one another as though they were attempting a futile embrace.

Kø sat down on the unfamiliar white sand and looked out at the natural bay that had shielded him from the ocean's heaving waves. Beyond him, the ocean presented a barrier, a chasm, a yawning void between Kø and his happiness, his fulfillment, and his future. A breeze teased his hair and tossed it into his eyes.

Unfeeling, Kø ignored it. He looked but saw nothing. He touched but felt nothing. Nothing had meaning anymore. He lay on his back and looked at the stars. The stars relayed nothing about the destiny he so believed in. He thought about the three most important people he had left behind, and hot tears scalded his eyelids and burned a path down his cheeks. Anxiety gnawed at him like oversized rats that gnaw on sugarcane. How was he going to get off the island? How could he get to Denmark to see his father? How would he go home to Quitta, to Eva, and to his mother? No matter how hard he tried, he couldn't stop the tears…there was absolutely no way of escape.

14

Many miles away, Evado laced her fingers protectively over her ever-growing midsection. Her heart was heavy as she watched the hot sun rinse the clouds in the orange rays of sunset. And when night clothed the clouds in dark, somber, funeral clothes, she raised an incessant lament to the father of her unborn child....

Kondo yi yevuwo de me gbo ee

Kondo has gone to the land of white men....

After all this time he isn't back yet...

She sang it over and over again, and she felt her tears would never end.

Metrova, Kø's mother, busied herself all night. She and a dozen or so of her staff had a lot of work to do to get produce ready for the market, and food prepped for her restaurant. With all the hustle and bustle, Metrova had no time to think about her son and all the other issues that terrorized her at night. In fact, she tried very hard not to think about him. However, at the darkest side of dawn, her stomach constricted painfully and deep inside her, she began to feel her son's anguish. She held her head and rocked herself from side to side. She knew, as only a mother knows, that her son was in deep trouble. As if in telepathic harmony, Metrova echoed Eva's words as tears of helplessness ran down her cheeks. Sobbing, Metrova ran out of her home to the beach. Her feet led her to the spot where she last saw her son. There, circling the spot, was Eva, protecting her midriff, singing the song.

Kondo yi yevuo de me gbo ee

Kondo has gone to the land of white men....
After all this time, he isn't back yet...

Metrova held tightly onto Eva.

Kondo yi yevuo de me gbo ee
Dada be mina mitsogbe d'edzi.....
Kondo yi yevuo de me gbo ee
mitsogbe d'edzi.....

Kondo has gone to the land of white men....
After all this time he isn't back yet...
But, his mother swears that he will come back
I, his mother swear... he will be back!

They sang and danced the age-old dance their ancestors danced when they broke free from that cruel and oppressive King[15] hundreds of years earlier – two steps forward, one step backward, three steps forward, one step backward, they danced. Though she sang the songs of freedom, her son's anguish tore at her heart and the pain was more than she could bear. Metrova regretted asking Kø to go and find his father. He needed it. But she needed him, and she needed him back alive. Maybe he was dying or dead. She clung onto Evado weeping. Suddenly, her clutch became lax. The weeping ceased.

"What's wrong Mama?" Evado asked as Metrova began to slide out of her arms.

"Mama!" she cried. There was no answer.

"Mamaaaaaaa!!" she wailed as Metrova lay lifeless in the sand.

---

[15] Torgbui Agorkoli was a tyrannical ruler of Notsie, a town in southeast Togo, West Africa. When the Ewe people decided to escape his rule they passed through a crevice made in a thick wall and walked out backwards, to confuse their pursuers.

125

PART 2

15

It was a breezy morning, three months later, when Kø reclined in an old easy chair, half asleep, under a huge flamboyant tree. The tree was in full bloom, and its bold red flowers adorned it like an ostentatious crown. For once, Kø relaxed. He loosened the buttons of his shirt, and the breeze played with the fine hairs on his chest. Boussy and his entourage of about two dozen people arrived. For a delegation so large, they were so soft-footed that Kø was startled when he heard a familiar booming voice just a few feet away from him:

"There you are, my friend; my brother from another mother!" Boussy said loudly. "You're looking mighty fine! god Lisa really saved you!"

Kø roused himself, straightened his shirt and looked at his new friend with mild annoyance. They were about the same age, but they were as different as charcoal and ash. Somehow, there was an affinity that neither man fully understood. So Kø graciously cleared his furrowed brow and welcomed his new friends. Boussy pulled up a chair and sat beside Kø. Those who could find chairs pulled them up while others sat on overturned boxes or in the sand. They cast curious glances at Kø. His story had not yet been told, and they couldn't wait to find out who he was, where he came from and how he got to their island.

"Tell me, Boussy, why do you refer to God as 'Lisa'?" asked Georgie one of the two boys who found Kø at the beach.

"Yes, why, Boussy?" asked the other boy, Lucky. "Lisa is a girl's name!"

Georgie and Lucky were best of friends. They were about ten or eleven years old and were the same height. They were born just a few days apart but in the same month and they looked like brothers. They were both brown skinned and had a generous sprinkling of freckles. Strangely, they didn't look anything like their parents or their siblings, and no one really understood why. People who saw Georgy and Lucky together shook their heads.

"Only mothers know!" people exclaimed.

Kø liked the two boys. They were energetic and always up to something. They reminded him of himself when he was young. They looked from Boussy to Kø and back again waiting for an answer.

"God was described as male by Europeans," said Boussy. "But how would one know if God was really male or female?"

Those present shook their heads, and Boussy continued.

"Has anyone seen God to prove that He is male? To us, God is neither male nor female and yet, he is both! *Sogbo* is the masculine spirit of God and *Lisa* is the feminine spirit.

"To us," Boussy concluded, "but more importantly, God is timeless, powerful and eternal. We call God *Mawu Sogbo Lisa.*"

"*Sogbo Lisa?* **Mawu** *Sogbo Lisa?*" Kø sputtered, surprised. "How? How do you know this? Tell me how!"

"Why? What's wrong?" asked Boussy, alarmed.

"Tell me how you know about *Mawu Sogbo Lisa?*" Kø asked again fixing him with an intent look. "How come you know the name? I thought you were born here!"

"No, Kø! I was born in a town called *Denu* on the Guinea coast!"

128

"Denu isn't far from Quitta, where I come from!" Kø exclaimed, shocked.

"I actually know where Quitta is," said Boussy, "and most of the people sitting here were brought from that same town or its environs!"

"*E du dzea?*[16]Do you still remember the language?" Kø asked.

"*Me du dze,*"[17]Boussy answered, "I still remember the language."

"*Mie du dze,*" echoed several men and women in the entourage.

"We understand the language," they said.

Suddenly, the enormity of what had taken place hit Kø between his eyes. Unbidden, tears ran down his cheeks. Never did he imagine, when he started his journey, that he would meet his fellow countrymen in such a place. An island of no return. A place where he could see the result and the impact of the slave trade for himself. It had cruelly dislocated his people. The spurned were now the saviors. They could have been his neighbors back home. He might have met them in the street. They might even have been friends. And yet here, they met, in the most unlikely of places. No matter what Kø did, he was unable to stem the flow of tears at man's inhumanity to man. For

---

[16] The literal translation of this is "Do you eat salt?" The real meaning is "Do you understand my language?"

[17] Literal translation is "I eat salt."

a long time, most of those gathered there, wept silently with him, for him and for themselves.

"Life is the beginning

of death"

African Proverb

131

16

"I was thirteen when I was kidnapped and brought to the Caribbean," Boussy said softly. His eyes were red from weeping, and he blew his nose noisily.

"My father was the King of a town called *Denu,* and he had three wives. His first two wives had five daughters each. He married my mother because he was desperate to have a son. My mother had three sets of twin daughters before I was born. I was the last child and the only son out of seventeen children! So I was everything to my father, and he was everything to me."

"Goodness!" said Lucky counting the number of children using the fingers of both hands and finishing on both feet. "That's a lot of children to have!"

"It was normal in those days, Lucky," said Boussy. "And it was important for Kings to have many children."

"Well, I was the spitting image of my father. I behaved like him, I walked like him and talked like him. When he sat with the elders of his cabinet, I was never far behind. There was no question I asked that my father didn't answer. He taught me many things about how to govern and how to be a royal and even at that young age, he began to groom me to become a ruler someday."

"So, tell me how you got here, Boussy," Kø asked anxiously.

"My father, grandfather and great-grandfather were all slave traders." Boussy began in a low voice.

The onlookers exclaimed in shock.

"What! They exclaimed. "You never told us this!!!"

"Unfortunately, it's true," Boussy said mournfully.

"They had agents who raided the villages and towns for men, women, and children. They chained the captives and marched them for miles and sold them either at slave markets along the way or directly to the slave ships. In exchange, they bought goods from the European traders which they sold on the Guinea Coast. It worked out just fine between the two trading parties.

"One day, a white man called Mr. Whyte called on my father in his palace. My father knew him well and had had business dealings with him for many years. He told my father that the slave trade had been abolished and that he was about to retire. He invited my father, and about a dozen other chiefs over to his ship for a last feast. My father and the other rulers were delighted and honored the invitation.

Of course, rulers never travel alone, so each ruler came with his entourage of between half a dozen and a dozen attendants. I was so excited to be going on a ship that I did cartwheels in the sand! I asked my father a million questions and didn't allow him to answer any of them. He smiled and ordered fine clothes for us to wear for the occasion. He was the ever-indulgent father!"

"What did you wear?" asked George.

"Shhhh" several people silenced him. "Let Boussy tell the story."

"Mr. Whyte sent the ship's boat for us," Boussy continued without missing a beat. "People gathered on the beach and watched us with envy. They could just envisage the feast we were going to have. And indeed, what a feast it was! There were at least forty-five visitors, and we were fêted royally. Little did we know, that we were at *The Last Supper*! There was every drink under the sun, and Mr. Whyte made sure every adult there drank to the point of stupor. I ran up and down the ship looking at everything and asking questions and climbing into everything. Mr. Whyte asked me to take a sip of the drinks the men drank. After a few long swigs, I felt my head spin, and I fell asleep under the long dining table.

I woke up with a start when I felt I was being carried. I looked at the muscular, pockmarked sailor who carried me, and he didn't look back at me. I didn't know him, but as a prince, I was used to being carried, so I thought nothing of it. I put my arms around his neck and promptly fell asleep again.

It was the violent shaking of chains and the unusual terror in my father's voice that yanked me out of my slumber. The terror in his voice was amplified when the other kings and members of their entourage woke up and joined their terror with his. There were other men, women, and children in the hold of the ship. Their fate was the same as ours. The only difference was that they had been kept in chains in dungeons for months prior to being shipped off, so they had been prepared with the fact that they were going to be shipped off to a distant land and re-sold into slavery. Each and every one of us was stripped down to our underwear, and the thin sheet provided, covered our vital parts. We were chained so tightly to the bare floor that we didn't have the ability to sit, stand or turn if we wanted to.

The ship was in full sail, and you could feel the forceful forward movement and the slight soothing side to side motion. There were a few portholes that let in very little light and even less air. The air was stuffy and putrid, the stench, unbearable. A unanimous lament went up from the voices chained to the ground. Our angst touched the ceiling, bounced off and came back to us as an abysmally amplified lamentation. The more we wailed, cried for mercy and begged for our freedom, the more the sounds echoed and amplified until it sounded like a dirge from a discordant choir conducted by Satan himself."

"Mr. Whyte! Mr. Whyte… you can't do this to me…" yelled my father at the ceiling.

"Mr. Whyte! I thought we were friends?" my father continued.

"This is *Boussou*! This is *Boussou*! Abomination! Abomination! We are people you can't enslave! We are royalty! You know this Mr. Whyte, you know you can't do this!" my father cried over and over again.

"Boussou!" he kept on saying. "Boussou! Boussou!! Boussouuuuuuu!"

"It was evident that salvation wouldn't come from above. Heaven was sealed shut and we quickly realized that we had to deal with our new hellish reality. To deflate our terror, we had to be silent; we had to internalize our pain, loss, and confusion. We had to swallow our fears. We had to blank our minds. We had to live each within himself. We wrapped ourselves in nothing, but our outer skin as the ship swiftly sailed to complete our captivity.

Life or death was suddenly a choice that one could make if one rose to that level of consciousness. My father chose to die. It dawned on him that he, his father, his grandfather and the likes of him who had raided villages and kidnapped men, women, and children to be sold into slavery, had put his fellow men through the same ignominy. Now, it was his turn to feel the pain others had felt. As the journey progressed, my father lost his mind. He didn't even recognize me, his only son. Indeed, he became a gaunt old man I couldn't recognize.

One night, he found a loose nail from one of the floorboards and cut a vein in his wrist. He quietly bled to death. My father died without saying anything to me. He never spoke to me directly once we woke up in shackles. Maybe it was his guilt; I don't know. I believe he called on Death and Death mercifully answered him. His blood was never cleaned, and those that slept near him slept in his blood for the entire journey.

I was not allowed to embrace him, pray for his soul, look at him or say my final goodbyes. Two sailors unchained his emaciated body. As they roughly picked him up, the cloth that provided him a little privacy fell off, and my father, the king, was carried out naked, without reverence for his station and without ceremony.

137

Death is a very important part of living in the African tradition. All his life, my father thought he would be buried with the pomp and pageantry of his predecessors. He thought he would be mourned for many days while the elders pondered on important succession issues. He thought his subjects would be shorn, wear black, walk barefoot and bury him with gold and precious ornaments and in utmost reverence. He thought that in death, he would be revered as one of the ancestors and that whenever men prayed, they would call his name and remember him. Instead, he was thrown overboard, naked as the day he was born and fed as fodder for the fishes of the sea.

I was inconsolable albeit for the shortest possible time…because the sound of my anguish trebled and amplified as it touched the ceiling. And the sound of my amplified anguish came right back to me as I lay there and hit me over and over again as the echoes churned around me. I quickly swallowed my sobs and willed myself to feel nothing. At least, I thought to myself; my father died a free man. He would not suffer the fate I was going to suffer.

It wasn't being sold, which happened later, that made me a slave, it was being on that ship. It was the way the journey tore at my soul and devoured my humanity that turned me from favored prince to a thing without essence.

I don't know if I made a conscious effort to live or die or if the choice was made for me. All I know was that I went to sleep when I did and woke up when I woke up. I ate when they fed me. I breathed because my breath came and went. My fate...my life was out of my hands!"

"Stop!" shouted Kø. "Stop, stop, stop! I can't take this anymore!"

"But this is what happened, Kø. This is the truth!"

"This is what we did to one another," Boussy said. "And this is what we allowed others to do to us."

Everyone was silent. Even the children were silent. Emotions could not be defined or explained. Thoughts and unexplained emotions churned in everyone's mind and soul.

"You know," started Kø, "back home in Quitta, we had slaves. But we never chained them. They worked hard, but they lived with us, ate with us, intermarried and even became part of the family. I believe we all thought it would be the same out here. We never imagined that the journey would be so dismal, so devastating and so degrading. We never imagined this torture! Never! Never!!"

Kø got out of his seated position and held his head. The pain he felt was unbearable. He knelt before Boussy and held his feet in supplication.

"As I kneel, Boussy, I represent all my people who collaborated to do this. I'm sorry for everything we did to you, Boussy." He turned and faced all those who were there with them that day.

"I apologize to all of you here who were brought in the same way. I apologize for the pain you went through. I apologize on behalf of all my people."

"You can't take the blame, Kø… you did nothing. My father engaged in it also. Maybe it was retribution."

The sun was beginning to set. Still, everyone sat still, waiting for something. People who had gone to work that morning were just returning. They saw the somber group and joined them. People huddled close to one another as the night air cooled them. Someone set a bonfire, and someone else brought breadfruit which they roasted and shared among themselves.

"How did you get to the Island of St John?" Kø asked Boussy. "Was that where the ship first docked?"

"I was bought by a plantation owner. His plantation was in St John, and that's how I got here. After I had been purchased, the plantation owner asked me:

'What's your name, boy?'"

I was about to mention my name when Mr. Whyte's agent said:

"His name is Boussy. His father calls him 'Boussy.' And that is how Boussy became my name. It's a constant reminder that my father's collaboration with Mr. Whyte to sell our people into slavery was in deed and in fact "*Boussou*" an abomination!"

Each person recalled how they had been bought, sold and resold. They showed the scars of injustice that their bodies still bore. But the unseen scars of mental confusion and self-loathing that left an indelible mark remained hidden just beneath the surface of their lives. It was morning when the last stories were told, and the cathartic night left everyone spent.

17

Kø knew that he didn't belong on the island. He was imprisoned there by circumstances, and he hated the state of uncertainty he found himself in. Worst of all, he just didn't know what to do about it. He walked to Haulover Bay and navigated his way over the rocks to Leinster Bay. Night called to him, and he answered willingly. Mindlessly, he allowed his feet to precede him down a wide path into the lush hills near the Sugar Plantation. The cacophony of insects' incessant whistling, buzzing and chirping filled the night. Kø heard nothing. Nothing could distract his feverish thoughts.

The old Moravian church loomed in front of him, and he stopped at the century-old church and wondered if there was a God in there. He stared at the red roof and pale-yellow walls and hoped that there was. He was badly in need of some divine assistance. He walked over to the East End of the island and stood at the beach, listening to the surf as it came and went. The air was fresh and cool and the vegetation behind him, lush and verdant. The smell of sugar and rum hung in the air. As he turned and walked to the hills, he could smell life.

It was the hooting of the owls that made his blood curdle. To him, owls were bad luck. Surely, there could be no bad luck greater than the awful dilemma he now faced. He soldiered on, actively listening to the sounds around him - the flap of bats' wings as they settled upside down on trees and the scurrying of small four-footed rodents looking for nightly sustenance.

He thought he saw light as he skirted the Plantation. He followed the light, cursing when he stubbed his toes on jagged rocks that protruded from the earth. The path was so unpredictable that he finally paid attention. Kø saw the light clearly now and realized that sitting on the cliff side of the promontory of Francis Bay was some sort of a fort surrounded by tall trees. He made his way up the steep incline to the side of the fort. About four feet from the walls were bramble and other thorny plants that made it impossible to touch or scale the walls. Evidently, the owner didn't want any surprise visitors. In the far distance, a ship was berthed. A few lights shone from its portholes.

"It was a much smaller ship than *The Pharaoh*," he thought to himself. "I wonder whose ship it is and what it's doing there."

He stood looking at it for a long time and suppressed the feelings that emerged as he thought about his father's ship. The moon shone dully as Kø carefully picked his way around to the other side of the fort.

Suddenly, the hairs on the back of his neck prickled, but before he could react, two hands gripped his upper arms in a vice, and a bright lantern shone in his face.

"What do ye want 'ere?" a gruff voice asked roughly.

Kø was so startled that he was at a loss for words. They shook him roughly.

"What do ye want 'ere???" Insistent voices rose several decibels higher.

"I...I.... I just wanted to walk." He tried to break free of the vice-like grip on his forearms, but they tightened even more.

"Well, ye're trespassin'!" they said gruffly.

The goons half dragged, and half hauled him into the fort with Kø protesting all the way. With the large door firmly locked behind them, they tied his both wrists behind him and left him standing. Kø looked at his surroundings. There was no light but moonlight from above and nothing but walls on all four sides of the courtyard. There were two sturdy, metal doors almost at right angles to each other. Kø decided to sit by the entryway. At least he knew that that door would lead outside and back to where he had come from. He sat on the uncomfortable, bare floor and waited.

It was daybreak when the second door finally burst open. Both Kø and the big redhead were shocked to see each other again.

"It's you! T' man o' t' sea! *You're a wee scunner!*[18]" Peegee exclaimed.

"Sir, Peegee, sir!" exclaimed Kø, smiling with relief.

"Untie him, untie him!!" shouted Peegee at no one in particular. There was a hive of activity behind the door, and a couple of men came hurrying out. They cut Kø free, and the big redheaded pirate clapped him on the back. Kø flushed when the unwanted image of the pirate's nakedness during his escapade with Daffodil flashed before his eyes. The pirate, however, seemed to have forgotten all about it. He led him to a long room behind the door. And there, behind the long rectangular table sat about three dozen men of various ages and sizes. The table was laden with food, and exotic drinks.

"Sit!" ordered the redhead.

Kø sat.

"This is the man o' t' water I told ye all abou'," he told the men. "His name is Kø. He is a friend, hopefully, not a foe," he said looking at Kø quizzically.

---

[18]Scottish for "You're a nuisance!"

"Friend!" said Kø hastily. "Definitely a friend!" he added nodding emphatically.

The meal was long drawn out; the conversation was filled with their escapades and the loot they had gotten on their many pirating trips. They talked about their women whom they left in Scotland and laughed uproariously as they discussed their favorite prostitutes on the island.

Kø ate heartily, drank sparingly and listened intently to all they said. The more they ate and drank, the more their tongues loosened.

"So, you're from Africa?" a man sitting next to him asked.

The man was totally bald with big protruding eyeballs. His eyes were permanently reddened, colored by an excessive indulgence in rum and cannabis. He had a thick salt and pepper beard he had braided and secured with bits of ribbon in three separate parts. When he opened his mouth to speak, which wasn't often, all you saw were eight missing front teeth. The rest of his teeth were an indeterminate red-brown color, permanently stained from chewing tobacco. As you looked into the gaping hole in his mouth, all you could think of was, that this must be a highway through the flames of hell.

"Yes, I am from Africa," Kø said looking down at his food.

Everyone stopped eating suddenly and turned their full attention to him.

"You 'ave to tell us wha' 'appened to you, Kø," interjected Peegee. 'You have to tell us how you got here."

"I will, sir. Peegee, sir," said Kø simply.

18

"We were sailing from the Guinea Coast, to Denmark on my father's ship, *The Pharaoh*," began Kø slowly, "but we had to make a stop at the Virgin Islands to buy some sugar and rum.

"There were two things I wanted above anything. The first was to see my father and the second was to learn how to sail a ship. Sailing my father's ship was my childhood dream, and I was so determined, that the Captain and the boatswain, Johan, taught me everything.

The day we encountered the hurricane was frightful, and many sailors got hurt. I had worked for eighteen hours straight because we were so shorthanded. By the time I finished work, I was so tired that my cabin seemed too far away. I promptly went to sleep in the ship's boat.

Kø sat back, his eyes took on a faraway look....

"That night, I dreamed about Eva. The dream was so real, I thought she was lying beside me.

"Katie.... Katie!!" a man called out.

The voice suddenly jolted me from my deep slumber. To my surprise, a woman lay next to me.

"Eva?" I said groggily.

"Shhhh! Please, please keep quiet!" the voice whispered urgently. I recognized it instantly as Katie's voice.

"Who is Katie?" a pirate asked.

"*Haud yer wheesht!*[19]" Peegee said harshly. And the rest of the story was told without interruption.

"Wha...What are you doing here?" Kø asked in astonishment.

Katie put her fingers on his lips, and he swallowed his question. Staccato footsteps came. She held her breath and lay perfectly still. Confused, he mirrored her actions. Staccato footsteps slowed, a man's boots scraped the deck as the owner of the boots turned this way and that. Footsteps gathered momentum. Boots left in a hurry. Silence returned. Katie let out her pent-up breath. Kø followed suit. Her eyes were huge and luminous, vulnerable and blue. The naughty girl was nowhere in sight.

"That's my husband," she said.

---

[19] Scottish for "Hold your tongue!" or "Be quiet!"

It was obvious. He was the only one who wore his soldier's boots on the ship.

Kø looked at her. The questions in his eyes were clear.

She turned away; there were tears in her eyes. He noticed that her dress was torn at the shoulder. He turned and gave her a brotherly hug. She put her head on his shoulder and sniffled.

"The matter between you and your husband is really none of my business," Kø explained to her. "I can only advise you if you want me to.

You may have heard this saying… "Advice is a stranger," He said lapsing into *Ewe*, their shared language. "If he is welcome, he stays for the night: if not, he leaves the same day."

Three sets of urgent footsteps intruded their conversation. They stiffened, willing the footsteps to leave. Footsteps left, and they continued.

"Aleksander, General Sønne, my husband is very jealous," she burst out. "I just can't seem to do anything right for him."

"You must understand him and be patient, Katie. He is much older than you are, and you are very beautiful and very young…"

"Do you think I'm beautiful?" she asked.

"Of course, you are," he answered, laughing. "Even a blind man can see that!"

She giggled, put her arms around him and gave him a kiss on the mouth. In the middle of that friendly kiss, the tarpaulin that covered the jolly boat was yanked off. There, stood an irate, red-faced General and two hefty men who had worked with him as his bodyguards at the Castle. They had yanked the tarpaulin just in time to see the Kiss. The General was so angry; he hauled Kø out of the boat as though he was some mangy dog and threw him at his henchmen.

Kø paused, shook his head at the memory.

"How dare you?" the General bellowed at me. "How dare you kiss my wife?"

His fists clenched and unclenched. I could hear his labored breathing, and a tic twitched his left eye. The henchmen held both my arms. The General came close, and I could see spittle form at the side of his mouth. Before I could give any explanation, he gave a blow to the side of my face. I could feel blood pouring out of my nostrils.

"How dare you?" he screamed again. His fists pounded my ribs and winded me completely.

"Don't, Aleksander!" Katie pleaded, holding his arm and trying to prevent him from hitting me again.

"I did nothing," I said to him when I found my voice "Please believe me. I did nothing to your wife!"

"Liar!" he roared. "Liar!! I saw you! I saw you with my own eyes!"

"Please believe him!" cried Katie. "Believe **me,** Aleksander!"

It was as though he heard nothing his wife said to him. He gave another blow to my jaw. The General waved his hands. It was a signal to his men. One of them held my feet, and the other held me under my arms. They picked me up as though I was a sack of corn and they carried me to the side of the ship.

Out of the corner of my eye, I saw my brothers. They were huddled together, as always, and were in the middle of a very animated conversation. Katie's husband lit his cigar while he held tightly to a weeping Katie. Her hair was disheveled, and she was trying unsuccessfully to right her disheveled clothes, while earnestly attempting to explain what had happened. Her husband's eyes were filled with jealousy and hatred as he watched me. The men picked me up and swung me to the left, and I screamed.

"Help me, please!" I cried in desperation. "Harald, I did nothing. Ask her...Ask Katie!"

The men swung me to the right toward the side of the boat.

"Harald! My brothers! I'm innocent! Help me! Please!"

The men swung me to the left.

"Am I not your brother? Do we not have the same father? Tell them to stop this!"

In the split seconds that remained of my life, I listened out for one word – **STOP** – from any of my brothers. Sadly, I heard nothing but Katie's wailing.

The sailors swung me toward the side of the ship, and the last sound I heard was Katie's blood-curdling scream.

"Noooooooooooo!"

"The balmy night air embraced me so tightly; it whisked my breath away. As suddenly as it embraced me, it dropped me as though I was an unpleasantly hot object. The ocean simultaneously opened its arms and encompassed me, pulling me to its watery depths as it had done to countless unfortunate people in generations gone. With everything I had, I refused its embrace. My legs kicked against the current and I surfaced spitting out salty water. I found air and drew it in, deep into my lungs, gasping and shivering with shock and fright. I swam toward the ship. It was a hopeless action, and I knew it, but I did it anyway, taking long, powerful, determined strokes toward the lantern I had put on the poop deck. No matter how hard I tried, I couldn't catch up. *The Pharaoh* sailed away, and eventually, I could no longer see the lights. The ship left me behind...... left me in the middle of the ocean.... left me to certain death.

The night was pitch black. The sea without color. I didn't know which direction to swim, but I willed myself to be calm. I thought about my mother, my Eva, my father and the hopes I had for my future. My tears mingled with the sea water. My arms were getting tired, and it was becoming useless to swim. I lay on my back and let the water carry me. I had been falsely accused, falsely condemned, and doomed to a watery grave.

The prayers of my forefathers came to me:

The SUPREME BEING

who is superior to all,

SOGBOLISA,

the one who is the embodiment

of masculine and feminine spirits.

KITIKATA

the one who created the microcosm from the macrocosm.

The one who out of the formless heavens created the earth

The great and overall God

The great craft person who creates hands and feet

Let my hands touch your creation and let my feet touch earth....

The prayers I had been taught in the church were on my lips:

Our Father, which art in heaven,

Hallowed be thy name,

Thy kingdom come,

Thy will be done on earth

As it is in heaven....

My mind wandered...

My life passed before me like pictures in slow motion...

The first picture was the one that stayed with me. It was the picture of my father. My earliest memory of him was when I was about two or three years old. I was ill with measles, and my mother was beside herself with worry because my fever wouldn't break. My father put me in his bed and watched over me all night while the fever raged. I threw up all over him when he fed me the vile concoctions my mother had prepared. Lovingly, he wiped my mouth, my brow, and the vomit.

Papi laid me under the crisp, white mosquito net that hung over his huge bed. I could smell the starch from the white bed linens and the slightly fishy smell of the sea that came from the large open window. I inhaled the foul smell of herbal concoctions, the chalky smell of calamine lotion on my skin and deep smell of brandy and cigar on my father's breath. These are the smells I always associated with my father. To me, those were the smells of love. Of unconditional love. It was only when the fever broke that my father came to bed.

"Kø-pigen, *min kære søn,* my dear son," he added a Danish word of endearment to my name. "You will be well now."

155

"Pa-pigen," I said transferring the term of endearment meant for a child to my father. I smiled weakly at him and trusted that because he said I would be well, that indeed, I would be well. He lay on one side of the bed; my mother lay on the other side. And with me cocooned in the middle, we slept.

The other pictures paled in the background. I didn't want to remember. I lay there mindless, looking for a star in the sky, looking for clouds, looking for anything that signified life. The night was soundless except for waves that lapped gently as they joined and parted. I don't know how long I lay there, clinging onto those memories of long ago, when I heard faint tweeting sounds. Could it be a shark I thought? I refused to think about its teeth tearing me apart. I looked at the black, unforgiving sky and silently begged for a few stars to break away the desolation. And yet, the sky remained so black, the sea so dark, there was nothing to give me hope.

Fortunately, the sea wasn't cold, but I could feel the salt from the seawater biting into my fingers and toes. Salt seeped into my ears and entered every crevice of my body. Despair dug its unrelenting fingers into me. As dawn began to break, I realized how alone I was, lost in the middle of the ocean. The waves were constant in their up and down and sideways motion. They

156

lulled me to sleep. I closed my eyes and willed death to take me. I really don't know if I slept or when I slept. When I finally woke up, I was here, in Daffodil's home."

There was a long silence. But finally, Peegee broke the silence; he measured his words carefully as he spoke.

"What are you doing now?" he asked me.

"Nothing," I said.

"So, do you really know how to navigate a ship?"

"I do."

"And do you really know how to shoot?"

"I do."

Peegee stroked his long red beard thoughtfully as he studied Kø.

"You may leave now," he said unexpectedly.

I didn't wait for a second invitation.

19

The sun hung just above the horizon, as though it had been suspended there by invisible threads, when a few people began to gather. Kø lounged on the white sands of the Salt Pond Beach with Boussy and Hololegs. Boussy had caught a large barracuda that evening. He scaled the fish, cleaned it and set it on hot coals. Hololegs brought some yams from his farm, and he stuck them into the embers of the fire, skin and all, and let them roast slowly. One by one, others began to join them.

By the time the invisible threads relinquished their hold on the sun, there were about two dozen people sitting around the fire eating and talking. It was a luxury they were not used to, but they embraced it as part of their new reality – their recently found freedom. Somehow, the conversation turned to Emancipation: the day shackles of bondage were removed from their necks, and the day they were able to breathe the sweet air of freedom.

"How did it happen?" Kø asked curiously. "Tell me how freedom came after so many years of bondage."

Someone stoked and added a few dry twigs to the edges of the fire.

"Do you remember the old saying that 'no matter how hot a thing is, it will definitely cool down one day?'" Boussy asked.

"It was time..." people murmured. "The time for freedom had come!"

"No! It was long overdue!" others said.

"Our people always wanted to be free," said an old man called Heze Kaya. He was well over eighty years old and was born into slavery. He was separated from his parents and sold as a child and remembered nothing of his parents. He was wiry and wizened, but he held himself ramrod straight, as though if he were to bend even a little, he would snap in two. His eyes were clear, his mind sharp and he held the oral history of their existence well preserved in his memory.

"We never accepted our state of enslavement, you know. Never!" he began.

The circle of people murmured their agreement. The circle was tight, but they moved even closer to one another.

"The struggle for freedom began in 1733, when there was a lot of hardship on this island," Old Man Heze Kaya began.

"A horrendous hurricane devastated the land, and after that, a terrible insect infestation caused drought on the island. Many slaves marooned. They ran away and hid in the mountains. On November 23, 1733, one hundred and fifty slaves who had been brought from Akwamu[20]rebelled. They killed their owners and took over their plantation at Coral Bay for six months."

After this, the story went on as though it had been choreographed. Randomly, the people contributed a sentence or two to the story. Kø realized that it was a collective story. A common experience, a shared history. He felt, in a way, privileged to be part of their history. Because their history had now become part of his story.

"We were told that that was the longest rebellion in the history of the Americas!"

"I heard that story," someone said. "I was on another plantation in St Croix."

"They would have been successful if one fort soldier had not escaped to alert the authorities," another interjected.

"I heard that soldiers had to be brought from Martinique to help the white owners."

---

[20] Akwamu was a state set up by Akan people (in present-day Ghana) that flourished in the 17th and 18th centuries.

"Where is Martinique?"

"Far away, but not too far."

"They speak French over there."

"When French soldiers came from Martinique to overpower them, most of the *Akwamu* committed suicide."

"They said they would rather die than be enslaved."

"So, through the ages, we fought hard," Old Man Heze Kaya took over the conversation again.

"Sometimes in open rebellion and sometimes in silence... We fought when cruel whips laced our backs. We fought groaning in prayer, we fought...."

"We can never forget when Emancipation finally came in 1848."

"It took almost a hundred more years before Emancipation finally came!" Kø exclaimed.

"It did!"

"It did!"

"But it came! That's what is most important!"

The old man dug into the recesses of his pocket and brought out an old newspaper cutting which he gave to Kø. The piece of paper was frayed and worn at the edges.

NEGRO EMANCIPATION

> **The Religious Services connected with the celebration of the THIRD of JULY 1848, as the Day on which Slaves of the Danish West Indies will receive the blessings of Civil Freedom, will be as follows: At Half-past Six O'Clock in the morning a Public Meeting for Thanksgiving and Prayer will be held.**

"I kept this as evidence, so if I was ever asked why I was not in the barracks I could show it as proof that indeed, I belonged to no-one! I finally belonged to myself!" Heze Kaya wiped his eyes and face with both hands. The joints of his hands were knotted and gnarled. They were old hands that had done more than their fair share of work. The many calluses bulged, reshaped and misshaped his hands.

The sense of shared history continued, when people once again began to randomly interject into the narration.

"I couldn't believe that Emancipation finally came!"

"God answered our prayers."

"Yes he did!"

"Don't be fooled! The plantation owners started to lose money! That's why they set us free!

"Yes, they couldn't feed us anymore."

"Really?"

"Whichever way it happened, I think God had a hand in it!"

"But the fact is, that we were emancipated. We were set free!"

"It was very difficult."

"Yes, it was. We negotiated to work for the plantation owners."

"We asked them for weekends off!"

"They didn't like that at all!"

"No, they didn't. But we wanted to go to church on Sundays."

"And we stayed in church all day on Sundays..."

"So we needed Saturday off to take care of our families and our needs."

"They said it was unheard of...."

"But we got the days off anyway...."

"Till they couldn't sustain their plantations anymore."

"So here we are now."

"It's been difficult."

"But even after two years, I still feel unspeakable joy!"

A look of pure bliss settled on everyone. From somewhere in the back, a voice raised a song:

> There is a balm in Gilead
>
> To make the wounded whole;
>
> There is a balm in Gilead
>
> To heal the slave-sick soul.[21]

The old man continued:

---

[21] African-American spirituals

"This is what it means to be free. I can sit here with you and eat what I want to, rest when I want to, and even sleep when I want to!"

"Yes... and I can marry whomever I want to," a young man said smiling. He was sitting with his arm around a young woman.

"And we don't have to fear that our children will be taken away from us while we are still nursing them!" an attractive woman said.

"Indeed, the day came... July 3rd, 1848."

"And from that day, we became the master of our own fates and the captain of our souls."[22]

"I had had a child a few years earlier," A young woman called Axelina said, "She was a beautiful girl and I named her Mandy. I was a cook on the plantation. The master took my child from me as soon as she started walking... and he sold her into slavery. Before he took her from me, I made a tattoo just beneath her right ear, so I would find her someday.

You see," she continued "we had heard that other slaves in places like Jamaica had been emancipated, so I had faith that our emancipation would just be a matter of time. Once we were emancipated, I walked to all the five plantations on the island. I

---

[22] A quote from a **poem** "Invictus" by the English poet **William Ernest Henley** (1849–1903)

found my daughter! I found my child. Here she is! Here she is! This is Mandy!"

She hugged her seven-year-old daughter closer. There were tears in her eyes, but her smile was broad, proud and triumphant.

"I remember, after all the speeches at the church, we went to the highest hill on the island and faced east," continued another man. He was a quiet man called Ezekiel. He never seemed to have much to say.

"We refused to sit or sleep all night because we were told that Freedom would come with the rising of the sun.

"We were told that we would never have to live our lives under the violence of scourging whips or under the constant threat of death."

"So we stood.....all night!"

"All night we waited for the Sun of Freedom to rise and shine on us!"

"And surely, the following day, the sun rose from the east, from Africa! And as the Sun of Freedom rose, we knew, that at long last, we were truly a free people!"

"Yes," said Boussy. His voice was not loud, but it carried beyond the circle of friends. "Emancipation Day was joyful indeed. I wept with mixed feelings. I couldn't help it, you know... I remembered my father who died on the way here; my mother, my sisters and my home....I asked myself a few questions: was I free to go back to my home where they kidnapped me from? How could I go back home to the land of my birth? How would I ever get back to my people? Even if they gave me a ship, how would I find my way back? With all these thoughts going through my mind, Emancipation Day was bittersweet for me."

"If you could go back to Africa, would you go back?" asked Kø.

"I most certainly would!" Boussy exclaimed.

"Yes, I would!"

"I've never been... but I would."

"I would too!"

Every hand went up except the old man's. There were tears in his eyes when he spoke.

"My years on earth are almost finished. My time is almost done. It is the young who should go. They have something to contribute when they go back. I prefer to be buried in the land that took my life, my dreams and my hopes. They can keep my bones. I cannot let my people mourn my absence and burden them with my ailing, aged presence. I was emancipated too late. But this time is better than not at all!"

And they began to sing:

Emancipate yourselves from mental slavery[23]

---

[23] Derived from a speech given by the Pan-Africanist orator, Marcus Garvey, entitled "The Work That Has Been Done".

None but ourselves can free our minds!

After that day, Kø decided to make the best of his days. He had never experienced slavery, and he was grateful for that. The island was not a prison. Yes, he got there by a twist of fate, but after hearing all their stories, he learned that one must never give up hope. He believed that no matter how impossible things seemed to be, one must always cling to hope and work toward a goal. If slavery could be abolished after more than three hundred years, then one must never lose faith because everything is possible.

20

Kø took up carpentry again. He built a small home for himself in Salt Pond Bay surrounded by his new family. He opened his carpentry shop and made furniture, built new homes, and re-roofed the shanties if need be. Each morning, with the rising of the sun, Kø smiled with optimism. He was hopeful that no matter how impossible it seemed, he would someday, see his father, his family and his motherland.

After trying to keep up his optimism, Kø still had bouts of restlessness and despair that threatened his equilibrium. He had been on the island for over two years, and though he was getting used to his life with his new 'family' and friends, thoughts about his real family on two separate continents were never far from his mind. He was almost twenty-seven, and he still felt there was something missing in his life...Perhaps, he thought,

what he needed was a family of his own. A wife and children…
maybe that would take his mind off things.

He went down to his regular spot at Salt Pond Bay and sat on
the beach. He needed to think. The sliver of moon was darkly
luminous, giving off just an eighth of its light. The ebb and flow of
the Caribbean Sea was gentle and constant. Kø's brow furrowed
deeply as he pondered on the next trajectory of his life. But the
answers he sought didn't come easily. His restless feet led him
up the steep incline and into the mountains. He walked to the
coral and rubble rock-strewn beach of Lameshur Bay. He cursed
as he stumbled and stubbed his toes against the rocks and
remnants of cactus roots sticking out of the ground. He stood
on the hill and breathed in the fresh air.

Maybe, he thought darkly, he should forget about ever seeing his
father, mother and Eva, accept his lot and make a home here.
He took in the dramatic scene from his vantage point and
listened to the rhythm of the pieces of coral rolling back and
forth in the surge. Maybe he would have peace if he accepted
the hand that fate had dealt him. His thoughts led him up the
hills and into the Bordeaux Mountains until he found himself
close to the windmill at the Sugar Plantation. The plantation was
surrounded by stone walls and almond trees. He skirted the

169

plantation and walked eastward toward Francis Bay. There, in the distance, was the small ship he had seen previously. Kø's interest was piqued again, and he walked closer until he got to the edge of the cliffs. The ship had no sails, no flag on the mast, no name on its stern, no ornate carvings on its bow and no lights in the portholes.

His mind was so focused on the myriad of unanswered questions, that it was really too late when he sensed some movement behind him. Before he could react, two bald men with long beards and mustaches grabbed him in a vicelike grip. Not again! Thought Kø, gritting his teeth. Both men looked like they had forgotten how to smile, and they responded to Kø's perplexed greeting with a hint of a taciturn nod.

Without protocol, the men ushered Kø through the large doorway of Peegee's fort and ushered him directly to a small room where the big redheaded pirate was busily poring over maps. The only furnishings in the drab grey room were two straight back chairs and a table. The ceilings were very high, and the windows were tightly shut. The loud clang that reverberated all the way down the hallway, when Peegee shut the huge metal door, made Kø quiver inside, but he refused to let his countenance betray his fear and apprehension. After all, he had done nothing wrong.

The pirate sat and observed him without offering him a seat. Long minutes passed, and neither man said anything. Kø stood like a soldier, shoulders back, at ease, and arms loosely at his side. He had already faced death, so there was nothing else to fear. They assessed each other. Each man's expression inscrutable. Long minutes passed when suddenly the pirate said harshly.

"You know you are trespassing, don't you?" It was a statement rather than a question. "Sit down!" he commanded.

Kø slowly sat.

"I'm sorry, sir." Kø said, "I was lost in thought and didn't realize I was so close to your fort." Peegee looked at Kø intently stroking his fiery beard.

"I would like you to join us," he said.

"Join you?" asked Kø puzzled.

"*Yon's a right chancer!*[24]" said the Pirate, "I have observed you since I met you and I know you are hardworking, brave and loyal. We have an important operation coming up, and I would like you to join us." Peegee paused and picked up a folded piece of paper from the side table.

"Think about what I said. Let me know when you make up your mind."

---

[24] Scottish for "You are a risk taker."

"However," he continued, "these are our code of ethics," he handed Kø a piece of paper and demanded that he read it and hand it back.

Sitting down, Kø read the document in disbelief.

"Eleven Rules of the Pirate Code,"[25]

1. Every man shall have an equal vote in affairs of moment. He shall have an equal title to the fresh provisions or strong liquors at any time seized and shall use them at pleasure unless there is a scarcity.

2. If anyone defraud the company to the value of even one dollar in plate, jewels, or money, they shall be marooned.

3. If any man rob another, he shall have his nose and ears slit, and be put ashore where he shall be sure to encounter hardships.

4. No-one shall gamble.

5. The lights and candles shall be put out at eight at night and if any of the crew desire to drink after that hour, they shall sit upon the open deck without lights.

6. Each man shall keep his cutlass and pistols, at all times, clean and ready for action.

[25] thepirateking.com

7. No boy or woman shall be allowed amongst us. If any man shall be found seducing one of the latter sex and carrying her to sea in disguise, he shall suffer death.

8. He that shall desert the ship or his quarters in the time of battle shall be punished by death or marooning.

9. No-one shall strike another on board the ship, but every man's quarrel shall be ended onshore by sword or pistol in this manner: at the word of command from the Quartermaster, each man being previously placed back to back, shall turn and fire immediately. If both miss their aim, they shall take to their cutlasses, and he that draws first blood shall be declared the victor.

10. Every man who shall become a cripple or lose a limb in the service shall have eight hundred pieces of eight from the common stock, and for lesser hurts proportionately.

11. The Captain shall each receive two shares of a prize, all other officers, one and one quarter, and private gentlemen of fortune one share each.

"You shall be considered a private gentleman of fortune if you decide to join us," the Pirate said. "So you will be given one share. I give you twenty-four hours to decide 'Aye' or 'Nay'."

And then he snatched the document out of Kø's hand.

"When will the operation be, Captain?" asked Kø.

"I will only give you details if you agree to join us." And with that, Peegee turned and left, leaving the huge metal door wide open.

21

"Let's go fishing," Kø said to Boussy early the following morning.

Boussy looked at Kø, trying to read his mood. Kø's expression gave nothing away, so he gave up and led the way to Fish Bay where his canoe was berthed. It was only when he rowed out of the bay that he looked quizzically at his companion.

"What's on your mind?" Boussy asked.

Kø answered his friend's question with a question of his own

"Can we row round the island?"

There was silence in the canoe as both men concentrated on the task at hand. Water softly lapped at the sides of the boat, and the dip and the swish of the oars was all they concentrated on as they sailed their way round the island. Kø made sure they kept land in sight. After a long while, they saw a small ship moored between the promontory of Mary's Point, and a deserted island nearby called Whistling Cay.

"It's called at Bermuda Sloop or a man o' war," said Kø nodding at the ship. "It's much smaller than the ship my father had, but it will do."

"What are you talking about?" Boussy's high brow furrowed in confusion.

"Whose ship is this?" he asked looking at the ship and back at his friend. "What do you want to do with it?"

"Boussy," Kø said in a low voice. "Do you really want to go back home?"

Boussy looked at him in shock. Never did he think going back was a possibility. He looked at Kø wondering what was going on in his friend's mind. Kø met his gaze with all seriousness. Boussy realized it was no trick. This was real!

"I would love to go back to my people," Boussy replied.

Without warning, tears gushed from his eyes, and he let out a long loud wail. The tears he couldn't shed on Mr. Whyte's ship had been bottled in for so long. The dam of emotions that had been pent up for over two decades finally burst. Never in Boussy's imagination did he think it possible that he would ever make the journey back to his people. He didn't know the details yet, but what he was sure of what that he would be the first to know.

Boussy's chest heaved as he took in large gulps of air and tried to compose himself. He was embarrassed by his tears, and the veins in his neck seemed to inflate and deflate as he tried to choke back his emotions. Home... home.... Those words were so tantalizing. Dared he hope? Home! He had been away from home for a long time!

"How are we going to do this, Kø? How are we going to go home?"

Kø had a hard glint in his eye that Boussy had never seen before. His teeth clenched. His chin was firm. And for the first time, Boussy noticed the hard muscles of his friend's shoulders and arms. Kø's hands tightened around the side of the canoe and he said quietly:

"We are going to steal that ship!"

Long before the twenty-four-hour deadline was up, Kø made his way up to the Pirate's Fort. There was a light drizzle, but nothing was going to stop him from the morning's mission. No other decision was as important as this one.

For once, Kø looked round as if to imprint the island on his mind. He noticed the fire ants busily crisscrossing his path and he smiled. It was obvious that a little rain wasn't going to stop the tiny creatures either. Kø walked uphill through the

177

Bordeaux Mountains once again. He walked past the boiling house where cane juice was boiled in the process of making sugar, rum and molasses. The Age of Sugar was over, and the boiling house lay unused. That one house was the primary reason why Boussy and all the others were kidnapped from their homes. The owners of the boiling house had needed their labor. They needed free labor to grow and cart sugarcane from their vast farms to that house. The proceeds from the goods produced in that house made the owners so very wealthy.

Not far from there were the stone-built slave cabins. There were other houses that were made from mud and sugarcane thrash. In a clearing was a flat area called a bleach where laundry was laid out to dry. Though the plantation had been closed for almost two years, the smell of stale cassava still hung in the air. He supposed cassava was what the slaves were fed on. Kø sighed and quickly walked past the plantation.

It wasn't long before he got to his destination. This time no bald, hard, unsmiling pirates apprehended him. The main door opened as soon as he approached it and a ruddy, beefy guard at the entrance welcomed him in. The team nodded at him and ushered him to a long grey room, and there was an air of purpose that hadn't been there before. All thirty pirates had their heads together as they pored over maps and plans that were spread on the long wooden table.

Peegee greeted Kø with three words:

"...and your decision?"

Kø answered with three words of his own.

"Aye, sir!" he said with emphasis. "Aye!"

"You know the rules, spoken and unspoken," Peegee said. His voice resonated to include all those who were standing around the table.

"You know the risks and the rewards, and above all, you know the consequences."

"Aye!" Kø nodded solemnly.

The captain waved his hand, and everyone there understood that Kø was to be included in the circle of friends, and each pirate shuffled his feet as they made room for him.

"There is a Spanish ship going from Brazil to Spain with enough gold and precious cargo that will enable us all to retire in comfort. That is our target," Peegee began, pointing to Brazil on the map.

The plan to take the Spanish ship was ingenious. As the ship sailed close to the islands, they would attack its broadside so that it would be forced to change its course. By this action, the ship would run aground on a coral reef. Then they would attack and loot.

"The ship will be in the Caribbean in twenty-four days," Pirate Captain said. "We need to be ready in twenty-one days!"

Plans were made to procure guns and ammunition, food and water. Men were divided into groups, and each group was given an assignment. The men were to meet every day before dawn to exercise and train. The plan was marked with great thought and precision as Pirate Captain went over the plans again and again.

Hope and excitement welled in Kø's heart like a cascading waterfall in a rainy season!

22

Daffodil was agitated...really agitated. She knew something was going on, but she just didn't know what it was. Kø was suddenly very secretive, very aloof and he had a faraway look in his eyes these days. Her intuition told her there was something going on, and she was determined to find out what it was. Kø was like the big brother she never had, and she looked out for him the same way he looked out for her. When the hurricane destroyed her home last year, he built it from the ground up without taking a penny from her.

"One hand washes the other," he told her, sharing one of the many African proverbs and wise sayings he liberally sprinkled his conversation with.

"You helped me when I needed help, Daffodil, this is the least I can do for you." And he hammered away day and night and finished her house in record time.

She hoped that whatever was going on, he wasn't going to do anything stupid. No matter what, she was determined to get to the bottom of it.

Kø was in a tavern in Coral Bay making new chairs and tables to replace those that had been destroyed during a recent drunken brawl. Fortunately, he had just finished his contract, and he carefully counted and pocketed his fee when Daffodil breezed in with short quick steps. Her small, determined chin preceded her.

"Kø!" she called out to him in her singsong voice. She glanced at him, assessing him thoughtfully.

"What is it, Daffodil?" he asked.

"When are you going to tell me what's going on?" she asked directly, looking up at him.

"There's nothing..." Kø began.

"There is something..." she insisted.

Kø knew it was going to be a long argument. He took off in silence, taking long loping strides. She ended up running to catch up with him. Kø was standing in the middle of his house when she arrived. He had his feet firmly planted on the ground and his arms folded across his chest. Daffodil looked at him and knew that there was no way she would ever get the information she wanted out of him.

She planted herself in front of him.

"I have never told you why I sell my body," she said to him directly.

Kø was so taken aback that he gasped and sat down with a thump.

She ignored his reaction, sat down beside him and looked out of the window. A little distance away was a stone wall, abundantly covered with a creeping *coralita* plant. Its tiny pink flowers looked innocent and abundant. Daffodil concentrated on the flowers as she spoke.

"My mother was a mixture of many nationalities," said Daffodil. "She was a mixture of Portuguese, Indian, Danish and African. Her mother was a very beautiful woman, and she did the same thing I do now. She sold her body! She sold her body in order to make enough money to buy herself."

"What does that mean?" Kø asked puzzled. "How can one buy oneself?"

"There were only two ways a slave could be free. One way was by manumission, which is the act of an owner freeing his or her slaves. But that happened mainly if the slaves were old and the owner knew he couldn't profit from them anymore. The other way was only open to colored women. Colored women were allowed to pay the owners whatever their owners considered their price to be. The surest way for a colored woman to make money was to prostitute herself!"

"What?" exclaimed Kø.

Daffodil continued in her matter of fact voice as though she hadn't heard him.

"Colored prostitutes were and have always been in demand, and that was the only way open to women at the time. So rather than die a slave, my grandmother decided to be a prostitute. She paid the price, so all her descendants would be free!!"

Kø shook his head in disbelief.

"My mother and I lived in St Croix, the largest of the three Danish Virgin Islands," Daffodil continued.

"I didn't know that, Daffodil. I thought you lived here all your life!"

"We lived in Charlotte Amalie. Charlotte Amalie was a vibrant and beautiful city. It was full of merchants and sailors from Denmark, England and all over the world. There were many inns and taverns, ships and shops.

"One day, a Chinese man who had been stabbed, beaten and left for dead was brought to our home. You see, my grandmother had passed on the art of healing to my mother, so my mother stitched his wounds and nursed him back to health. Later, he and my mother fell in love. That's how I was born.

I was not even a year old when my father was involved in another altercation where he was stabbed to death. According to my mother, his corpse was found five days later. It was a very hard time for my mother and me, because apart from healing people, she had no other skills.

When I was about six or seven, a man was thrown off a horse not too far from where we lived. His leg was broken, and he was bleeding badly. They had my mother stem the blood flow while they got a doctor. That was how we met the wealthiest man in the Virgin Islands."

Daffodil paused and shook her head at the memories. Kø had learned not to interrupt Daffodil when she wanted to get something off her chest, so he waited.

"They never married, but he moved my mother and I into his home in Charlotte Amalie. And what a grand and beautiful home it was! We lived there for seven happy years. Or so I thought! Anyway, when I was about twelve or thirteen years old, the man I called my father raped me. He passed me on to his nephew when he was done, and it became a game they played. I was a mouse between two cats! My supposed stepfather threatened to kill my mother if I ever told her what had happened. The day my

185

mother found him raping me, he didn't stand a chance. She emptied every bullet from his gun into his body! We fled to St. John, but it wasn't long before the law caught up with her. Mother was tried quickly, sentenced and jailed. Nine days later, she was dead! They buried her before they told me about her death. I never knew how she really died, but I do know that someone from my supposed step father's family had had her killed. And I have been on my own since then."

Kø opened his mouth to say something. He was glad when she held up her hand and stopped him from speaking because he was at a loss for words. Daffodil tore her gaze from the *coralita* plant and looked directly at Kø in her disconcerting way.

"I don't want to remain like this forever, Kø! I don't want to be a prostitute till I'm old and used up! I want to leave this island someday, and I want that day to be sooner than later. I'm telling you this because I know you, and I know you're planning something. Whatever you're planning, if the plan involves leaving St. John, please don't leave me out. Please don't leave me here. Please take me with you!"

Kø sat for a long time in silence. Daffodil 'pinned' him down with her eyes till he gave her the answer she wanted.

"I promise you, Daffodil," he said solemnly, "if I decide to leave this Island, I will take you with me."

"I'd like to show something to you," she told him finally breaking her gaze from him.

Daffodil beckoned him to follow her, and she led the way to her home. She closed the doors and windows and pulled out the chipped, filthy looking chamber pot from under her bed. When she uncovered the contents, Kø was astonished at the assortment of gold nuggets, diamonds, precious stones, and money Daffodil had stashed away.

"I kept this, so I could one day buy myself a small inn or hotel somewhere. If you take me out of here, Kø, I will share this with you."

Kø's eyes widened, and he smiled a small, lopsided smile. He held out his hand, and she shook it.

PART 4

"One has to plan

how to run

and

also how to hide!"

Ewe Proverb

23

Boussy and Kø went out fishing again the following day when Kø asked, "Would you really board that ship and go home?"

"I would give everything to leave," Boussy replied earnestly.

"Then we shall leave in twenty days."

Boussy's eyes widened. Sweat beaded on his brow and ran down the sides of his face. He opened and closed his mouth several times in an attempt to find an appropriate response, but nothing came out of his mouth.

"Now listen carefully," said Kø. "I want you to select ten men and women that you absolutely trust. They must be determined to leave. We need men and women who can wield knife, cutlass and gun. We also need people who can cook, sew and paint.

Above all, we need people who realize that this is a top-secret mission and will keep their mouths shut."

"And Boussy, my friend," Kø said as he pulled the nets over the side of the boat and inspected the catch for the day,

"I want to meet everyone tomorrow at midnight. We will go fishing at midnight!" he said.

On the dark moonlit waters in one of the inlets at Hurricane Hole, three canoes bobbed gently. A hurricane lamp reflected dimly on the silent waters, and if one looked closely enough, one could see the blurred outline of eleven people. From time to time, a net was cast, so observers would assume that it was just a group of fishermen hoping for a good catch that evening. Eleven people anchored their canoes, huddled close together and spoke in whispers.

Boussy and Daffodil patiently sat in the first boat with Kø while he reached to the bottom of the canoe and picked up a sharp dagger and a bunch of dried reed. He sat back and waited for the others to settle.

In the second boat, Old man Heze Kaya sat ramrod straight next to Hololegs. He looked around at everyone and fixed unblinking eyes at the person who invited him there. Hololegs folded his long legs like a praying mantis at rest and rested his chin on his bony knees and observed everything with his usual mournful interest.

Opposite them sat Axelina, the mother of the tattooed baby. A reflective man of mixed parentage, Ephraim, a man of his word and a man of the Word, sat quietly beside Axelina. They looked good together, but they hadn't considered that yet.

A tall, dark, defiant looking man, King Mingo who was the leader of the Maroons, had come all the way from Jamaica with his assistant, Hunter. One could feel Mingo's raw, restless, palpable energy as he sat in the third canoe. Mingo lived in the mountains of *Accompong*,[26] in Jamaica. Fifty years earlier, when he was hardly a teenager in the savannah regions of Africa, he had wandered too far from his home. Despite his mother's warnings, he had a penchant for chasing lizards and pelting them with stones from his catapult. What he didn't realize, was that the slave raiders were on the prowl. They kidnapped him, chained him, made him walk the three-month journey to the sea and promptly sold him to a waiting merchant ship. He was ~~determined never to be en~~slaved. As soon as he arrived in

[26] Accompong (from the Akan name Acheampong) is a historical Maroon village located in the hills of St. Elizabeth Parish on the island of Jamaica. The people named their community Accompong after an early Maroon leader.

Jamaica, he managed to escape to the mountains. There, he found a group of other escapees (Maroons) who had set up residence there. He made Accompong his home, and after demonstrating much bravery and skill in the art of guerrilla warfare against their enemies, he became the leader of the Maroons.

Shippy, one of Boussy's friends, sat with them, and the three of them kept a plump well-endowed woman company. The woman sat on the broadest seat in the canoe. Her ample backside filled the seat completely and spilled over the edge just a little bit. She hunched over slightly so she could ease the pressure off her back as her ponderous breasts rested on her thighs. She was christened Anna, but everyone called her June Plum because she had an extreme fondness for the sweet, tangy fruit.

Kø cleared his throat and gently tapped the side of the canoe with the blunt edge of his knife to get everyone's attention.

"Our people back in Africa say, 'however long the night, the dawn will break.' The night of slavery was long and painful, but the dawn broke with Emancipation. The night of living here not knowing what tomorrow would bring is over now," Kø paused. "Another dawn has broken. An opportunity has opened for us to leave this island."

Ten pairs of eyes fixed on him and they held their collective breath. Kø continued in an even tone.

"We can leave this island in less than three weeks. And I have a plan as to how we can do this," he said.

"Three weeks!" a chorus of voices exclaimed.

Old Man Heze Kaya waved his bony misshapen hands, "How is that possible?"

"How can we leave?" asked King Mingo.

"It is possible," answered Kø. "It has become very possible!" he added excitedly.

Everyone started talking at once, asking questions and throwing in comments.

"Let him speak! Let Kø speak!" commanded Boussy. His loud voice silenced everyone.

"Before I tell you how," said Kø, "I need to know something. Is there anyone here who is not interested in going back home to Africa?"

"I am interested," said June Plum. She spoke up for the first time, "but I have many questions."

"If there's anyone who would rather not leave the island, they need to speak out now!" Kø said.

He looked at each man and woman in the eye, and one by one got agreement from every one of them before he proceeded.

"Back in Africa, our elders say, 'If an insect is going to bite you, it is already hiding in your clothing.' This means that the people closest to you are normally the ones most likely to betray you."

Kø lowered his voice, "This mission is and must be a top-secret mission. Do we agree?"

Again, he looked each person in the eye, and each person agreed.

"Can a person change his mind about leaving?" Ezekiel asked.

"No-one is forced to leave, you just need to ensure that you don't share our plan with people who might betray us."

"What do we do to anyone who chooses to betray us?" Boussy asked.

Kø unsheathed his dagger, and it glinted dully in the moonlight. The meaning was clear.

"How do we know that you are not taking us somewhere to be sold off again?" asked Mingo, the Maroon King.

"As you know, there is nothing in this world that is stronger than blood ties," he began. "People are bound together either by family ties or by the shedding of blood. This evening, you can become my family if you want to. I will fight for you, help you and protect you and if you agree to this, I hope you will do the same for me."

He took the knife in his right hand and pierced the fleshiest part of the palm on his left hand. Blood spurted from the wound, and

Kø held up his hand for all to see as the blood created a path towards his elbow.

"I swear by everything I hold sacred, that I shall never put you in harm's way here on this island, on the journey to Africa, or in Africa for as long as I live. Everything I have here, I will share with you. Everything I have there, I will share with you also. Your pain will be my pain, and your joy will be my joy, my people will be your people.

There was silence in all three boats as they reflected on his words.

"If anyone feels they do not want to be part of this, they need to state it now, so they can leave."

There was no response.

"If any of you wish to come with me," he said, "you will need to do the same thing that I have done. It is only then that we will know that we are in this by covenant and that we have one mind and one mission."

Without hesitation, Boussy took the knife. He cut a small part of his palm and clasped Kø's hand. Their blood mingled.

"I am with you, my brother," Boussy said.

His Adam's apple bobbed up and down as he swallowed his emotion.

Mingo, the Maroon king, followed suit. He cut his palm and clasped his hand with Kø's and Boussy's. Silently, all the women followed suit and then the men. The last man was the Old Man.

"Take me with you," said the old man cutting the palm of his hand. "And if I die on the way, promise me that you will bury my remains in my motherland!"

"I promise you this," said Kø.

"We promise," vowed the others.

Twenty-two hands clasped, one to the other. Each head was bowed in deep instinctive meditation. Blood mingled with blood, and new blood ties were formed. As blood oozed out of their self-inflicted wounds and dripped into the ocean, out of nowhere, lightning cracked a loud hole in the sky. Eleven heads snapped up and looked east.

Out of the hole, they saw the sound of thunder gather momentum from an abyss somewhere beyond the lightning and instinctively they were jolted backward. Lightning split the sky at three levels lighting the high heavens, the middle heavens and somewhere just above the sea. A vertical light held stubbornly, flickering and expanding. It was as though doorways were being made in the heavens. Thunder shot through each level. The lightning expanded and expanded again. Then, as suddenly as it started, there was darkness and a still, eerie silence. The motley group looked at one another. All they could hear was their own labored breathing. A new understanding dawned. Nature itself was a witness to what they had just done, and it seemed to approve, albeit vociferously, of their audacious plan.

"Even the heavens have condoned our trip," said Old Man Heze Kaya. It was half statement half question.

They nodded one to the other, still unwilling to speak.

"Indeed, God Himself has agreed to our move," whispered Ephraim.

"God is with us!" they whispered shaken by what they had just witnessed.

It was a long while before anyone spoke.

"But tell me," said Ephraim, "what is Africa like? What is Quitta like?"

A new authority resonated in Kø's voice when he spoke to his new family. He shared stories about his family back in Quitta and his Danish father.

"One thing I cannot do, is to promise you the world. But I do promise that I will not leave you or abandon you. We are in this together and will stay in this together.

There were discussions for a while as to what they might do when they get back to the land of their freedom.

Kø spoke up again.

Our people say, 'If you decide to run, you have to plan how to run. And if you decide to hide, you must plan how to do so.'"

Kø took a single reed and bent it. It promptly snapped in two. He bent the whole bunch this way and that, but the bunch remained unbroken.

"Together we can make this work."

"I remember my father used to say this all the time!" exclaimed Boussy.

"What you say about sticking together is the truth," King Mingo said.

"I cannot stress enough just how important it is for us to unite. Before we continue, we must agree, that if any of us has any doubt, any misgivings, any problem, any anger toward one another, we will address this calmly." Said Kø.

They all nodded in agreement.

"But above all, we have to plan strategically, and we have to plan now. As they say, if you plan to move a mountain tomorrow, you have to start by moving stones today."

It started to drizzle, but the eleven heads were too intent on their plans to bother about a little drizzle. The clouds covered the moon and gave them the cover of darkness that they wanted. Late as it was, every mind was alert, every heart, engaged, and every soul, in tune.

"Each person will be given a "stone" to carry so that we can move this mountain." Kø told them.

"I know what I can do," said June Plum suddenly. She sat upright and shifted her weight from one large buttock to the other, "the food of course!"

Everyone laughed.

"I will also help with the food," said Axelina. "You know I used to be a cook on the old plantation. I will dry, salt and smoke the meat and fish for the journey."

"I will hunt for deer," said Hunter. "And maybe we have to steal some cattle! Leave that to me!"

Old Man Heze Kaya knew where the caves were on the island. It was decided that everything they acquired would be stored in caves. Every day, items of food, clothing, ammunition and water would be taken to him. He would document everything, and when the time came, he would hand over everything to King Mingo, who would organize other Maroons to load the ship.

"Boussy," said Kø, "you and I will get the guns and the ammunition. We will go to St Croix for that."

"I can sew," said Ephraim. "What should I do?"

"I will give you the dimensions of the sails. We need to make new sails and craft a new flag."

"We will need cutlasses, knives, and axes, won't we?" asked Hololegs. "I will make those."

Everyone seemed to have things to do. Daffodil sat quietly. The only indication one had that she was thinking was the way she pleated and re-pleated the folds of her skirt. All eyes were on her because she was the only one who had not contributed to the conversation.

"Daffodil!" Kø called her, and she snapped out of her reverie.

"And I," said Daffodil, speaking slowly, "will get us everything we need to make our lives comfortable on the journey and in our new land."

"How many days do we have to plan all of this?" she asked.

"The countdown begins today," Kø said. "Today is day nineteen. We will leave in the evening on day zero."

"Do you know where the Greenville Plantation is?" Daffodil asked the group.

Everyone knew.

"I know that Plantation very well, and I know what the contents are and where they are. I need a group of at least twenty men to help me. We shall strip the Greenville Plantation of all its contents!"

Daffodil smiled a small victorious smile when she said, "And everything we take, we shall share."

"*We should count*

time

by

heart throbs"

Aristotle

Day 19

Kø took long, purposeful strides up the hill and vanished into the mountains. The pirates were expecting him for training, and he didn't plan on disappointing them. It was training that he desperately needed. For someone who had had absolutely no sleep the previous night, he was full of energy when he met Peegee and the other pirates for their daily workout. Kø was a man on a mission, and his adrenaline was pumping. He wrestled every man to the ground and hit the bullseye with every shot. Peegee was glad he had asked Kø to join them. The pirate stroked his long red beard and knew that he had picked a winner.

Daffodil went home and locked the door. She took the grimy, chamber pot from under her bed and emptied the contents onto her bed. Out tumbled various pieces of gold, diamond, ruby, pearl and turquoise jewelry. Not all the sets matched. Some were single earrings, and some of the brooches had a stone or two loose or missing. It didn't matter to her. She inspected each jewel carefully and separated them into two piles. There was an assortment of gentlemen's watches and rings. She put those into separate piles.

Then, she moved a heavy trunk out of the way. Under the trunk was a floorboard that had faint knife marks on one side of it. With a knife, Daffodil pried the board loose, and with some effort, hauled out a large roughly sewn burlap bag. She emptied the contents onto the bed. Gold nuggets, Danish Kroner, *Rigsdaler*[27] coins and notes made especially for use in the Danish West Indies, jangled as they tumbled out.

She inspected each coin to make sure the Danish coins were separate from the Danish West Indian coins. All the coins that carried the wording, "Dansk Amerik(ansk) M(ynt)", (Danish American Coinage), were put in a separate pile to distinguish them from regular Danish coins. She carefully grouped the coins into 6, 10, 12, and 24 skilling coins and grouped the notes as well.

She heaped all the gold nuggets into a separate pile by themselves. Then she brought out a small note book she kept under her mattress. It was well-thumbed, but each notation was carefully written with dates and other entries. She carefully checked everything to make sure all her treasure was intact. It was. With the money and all her treasures well documented,

---

[27] The RIGSDALER was the name of several currencies used in Denmark until 1875.

Daffodil lay back on her big bed, looked at the ceiling and began to dream of a new life.

Boussy rowed his canoe so hard that the veins in his arms stood out. Sweat streaked down his face and saturated his clothes. But there was no time for delay. Saint Croix, the largest of the three Virgin Islands and was not too far away, but after much thought, he decided to go to the Islands of Tortola and Puerto Rico to look for guns and ammunition to buy. He felt that people would be less suspicious. He rowed even faster!

Hololegs tried to keep calm as he thought out his strategy carefully. First, he surmised, he would spend his mornings on the farm so that he could harvest all his produce. Then, he would take everything to Axelina and June Plum to preserve. He was sure his wife would be happy to do whatever the two women couldn't handle. He decided to spend the afternoons and evenings making weapons. He had some scraps of iron in his workshop to begin work. With his hammer, anvil and chisel, he began to fashion out knives, daggers, axes and spearheads. He decided to make as many as he could each day. His long face looked even longer as he whistled tunelessly, but there was a new light in his eyes as he focused intently on the job at hand. He got out his bellows and fired up the furnace. Sweat ran down his forehead and into his eyes. He blinked them away, and his mournful look was suddenly transformed.

Old man Heze Kaya walked as quickly as he could behind King Mingo, and Hunter. For a while, he forgot all about the aches and pains in his bones and his joints. His mind was on nothing else but the matter at hand. He had children, inlaws, grandchildren and great-grandchildren. Granted he didn't know where they all were... some of them had been sold to other plantations elsewhere... but the ones that were close were precious to him. They were his family. His dilemma was how to get everyone onto the ship without causing suspicion and without word getting out. The more thought he gave to it, the more difficult it seemed. Maybe he might have to leave some of his family behind. This was going to cause him a lot of sleepless nights....

June Plum couldn't cook in her home. Cooking that much food would surely give her away. She knew that her man, Thomas, wouldn't want to leave the Island. It wasn't only because he had what was considered as a good job as a policeman, but also, because he had several children with several women. He loved those children and wouldn't want to leave them behind. What would he tell his children? How would he explain the situation to them? What would they tell their mothers? The situation was too complex. They had no children together - she would just have to leave Thomas behind.

"Can we make everything together in your home, Axelina?" June Plum asked when she went to visit Alexina later on that night.

Axelina had only one child, and she was free to come and go as she pleased. That evening, Hunter brought the first cow. Axelina and June Plum spent the evening cutting it into strips to make beef jerky. If June Plum had anything to do with it, she thought, no one would ever be hungry for three hundred and sixty-five days or however long it took to get to Africa.

Kø gave the dimensions of the sails to Ezekiel. He also gave him a quantity of rope and money to buy a few other items. The first thing Ezekiel bought was the sailcloth. He shut his door and pulled his large cutting table into the middle of his room. He got out his scissors and tape measure and cut out the dimensions for the twelve new sails and the new flag. On the new flag, according to Kø's express instructions, the word **Metrova** was to be painted on it. When Ezekiel asked what the word meant, Kø smiled.

"Metrova is my mother's name, but it means '*I have returned!*'"

As Ezekiel sat down to sew, he began to sing old Negro "*sperichils*". His voice was a surprisingly, deep, rich tenor that reverberated around the simple wooden room - and as he sang the tunes, the wounds in his soul began to heal.

Swing low, sweet chariot
Coming for to carry me home
Swing low, sweet chariot
Coming for to carry me home
If you get there before I do
Coming for to carry me home
Tell all my friends, I'm coming too
Coming for to carry me home

Day 18

King Mingo, his assistant, Hunter and Old Man Heze Kaya went to inspect the caves. They needed to make sure there would be adequate space for all their supplies and also enough space for almost two hundred Maroons who were preparing to leave with them. When Mingo got back to Jamaica the following day, he felt as though he had just woken up from a long nightmarish coma that had lasted fifty years. It was unfortunate that nothing could erase the deep furrows his constant frowning had etched between his eyes. With the new developments, however, he no longer walked as though he was trying to crack the earth open. The spring in his step was noticeable. He finally had a purpose and a plan for his life. Truly, nothing mattered to him more than getting everything right. He had one thing and only one thing on his mind – that each and every man, woman and child would get out safely if it was the very last thing he did.

Thomas went to June Plums home after work. The doors and windows were shut. He knocked on the door several times but there was no answer. It was not unusual for June Plum not to be home. What puzzled him was, that under normal circumstances, she would have told him if she was going to be out at night. Anyway, her laundry was hanging outside. She couldn't have gone very far he thought. He would come again the next time he was off from work.

Day 17

Daffodil looked at herself critically in the mirror. She liked what she saw. Her pale yellow gown was exquisite. It set off her dark hair and her caramel skin tone perfectly. And it showed off all her assets in the best possible way. When she stepped out that evening, her thoughts were on Mark. She hoped he would be in the tavern where she wanted him to be. As she stepped into the tavern, she held her head high, and curved her lips into a secretive, seductive smile.

Mark was seated in a shadowy corner, away from the bright lights, twirling the brandy in his snifter. Their eyes met when Daffodil entered the smoke-filled room, and he drained the glass in one large gulp. He grabbed Daffodil by the hand and led her outside without protocol. In a few short minutes, she was in the carriage with him, and Daffodil slowly unzipped his breeches and freed his member as though it was an unexpected prize. She kissed it, nibbled it, licked it and prolonged his sweet agony. When she had all but gobbled him, Mark was as high as a kite.

"Enjoy yourself," thought Daffodil as she worked her little pink tongue around him, "because before very long, you will lose everything you own!"

She smiled inwardly and continued her ministrations in earnest. Mark clutched the handles of the rocking coach tightly. He could feel the edges of both his wedding band and signet ring bite into his skin, but there were other more pressing delights to worry about. The delights came strong and sudden: He took a last look at the dark-haired beauty who knelt between his legs and tensed rigidly. After his release, he sank into the plush velvet seat of the carriage in utter contentment.

"Can we meet again tomorrow?" he asked.

Mark took out a large wad of notes and handed them to Daffodil. She gave him a kiss and tucked the notes between her breasts. He had become very taken with Daffodil. His wife was away in England, and he needed company. And Daffodil knew how to be great company. She was witty and bright, and she was a great lover. She knew just what to do, and he was very happy with her.

Mark was scheduled to leave for England soon to visit his wife and three children and he wanted to spend as much time as he could with Daffodil before leaving. He didn't care how much it cost him; she was worth it.

"Your wish is my command, my dear," Daffodil said with a winning smile.

Day 16

Shippy was reluctant to go to Daffodil's house. He didn't want people to think he was one of those that required her 'special services,' but he had to because she knew more about the herbs needed for healing various ailments than he did. So, he stuck out his chin and walked resolutely toward her house.

Shippy had lost an arm in a sugarcane crusher. He was feeding the sugarcane into the roller when the unfortunate incident occurred. He was fortunate that they stopped the machine when it got to his elbow. However, his right arm had to be amputated above the elbow, forcing him to become left-handed. That didn't stop him from doing whatever it was he wanted to. Today, he wanted to find every herb that might be needed for medication on the forthcoming trip, which was why he enlisted Daffodil's assistance. Together, Shippy and Daffodil went out to the mountains and valleys and to the banks of streams. There, they gathered leaves, seeds and roots for every imaginable ailment from scurvy to chicken pox and they made brews, ointments, and rubs to cure headaches, worm infections, wounds, skin rashes, diarrhea and fevers.

Day 15

Kø sat in his home and examined the various pieces of wood he had purchased. He got out his tools, and brow furrowed in concentration, he began to chip, carve, saw, sand and polish. In his mind's eye, he could see his mother saying:

"An army of sheep led by a lion can defeat an army of lions led by a sheep."

He whispered those words to himself over and over again until he believed every single word.

Then he thought of nothing but the job at hand. Everything had to be perfect. There would not be another chance to do anything over, so everything had to be just perfect!

Thomas was tired. He hadn't been home in three days. There had been several brawls over the weekend and he had to separate fights, lock up culprits and prepare them for court on Monday. It had been a tough weekend and all he needed was some hot food, a warm bed and the comfort of his woman. He couldn't wait to get to June Plum's home. He hadn't told her he was coming over, but he knew she wouldn't mind. He could swear he could smell her stewed oxtail and boiled banana specialty. And he could smell the sweet rose powder she used under her breasts and between her thighs. He doubled his footsteps.

Day 14

After training, Peegee gathered all the men together, and they sat around the long rectangular table.

"The first thing we are going to do is to clean out the ship tonight," he said.

"Then once we have our cache of guns and ammunition. We must make sure every cannon and every firearm is in place. We will need food, liquor, and other supplies," he continued. "And we will store items on the ship as we receive them."

"Will the things be safe there, Captain?" someone asked.

"From the time the first supplies are stored on the ship, we will have four guards stationed on it. We will have six-hour shifts, so our investments will always be guarded."

Everyone nodded in agreement.

"Aye, Aye, sir!"

Every Pirate excluding the four who were left behind to guard the fort went off to clean the ship, install the cannon, store the guns and ammunition and to practice in detail, how the operation was going to take place.

Day 13

Come with me," said Peegee to Kø, "let's go to the navigation room. I want to make sure you can sail this ship like you said you could."

Kø couldn't be more thrilled at the prospect.

The ship was built in 1843. It was just ten years old and was in great shape. It had a compass as well as a modern version of Harrison's Chronometer. It wasn't as luxurious as *The Pharaoh*, but it was fast and functional. Kø spoke without ceasing as he commented on the navigation system, the steering, the sails and everything he could remember.

Peegee took Kø through all the details on sailing the ship. They went over how to start the ship and how to moor it to anchor. They went over the setting of the mizzen masts, furling and unfurling of the sails and other numerous technicalities involved in sailing.

Peegee fired numerous questions at Kø.

"Do you know how to issue commands?"

"Can you command the ship by yourself?"

"How would you do this?"

"Can you steer the ship in case we are caught in a storm?"

"What would you do in this situation?"

"What would you do in that situation?"

Peegee was a hard taskmaster, but Kø loved every bit of it. He greedily lapped up every information he was given and performed every task with absolute focus and precision.

Peegee and Kø went on practice sails until Peegee was satisfied with Kø's dexterity. He was even more convinced that he had picked a winner. Kø was young, strong, daring and focused. Since Peegee invited Kø to join them, he had developed a certain fearlessness which was the one necessary ingredient for becoming a pirate. Kø also knew how to take authority and yet, submit to authority. Peegee was extremely pleased that he had recruited him.

Thomas couldn't understand it. He had visited June Plums home every evening for two days in a row. The doors and windows were firmly shut, and the curtains were drawn. There was no sign of life in June Plum's house. The laundry had been taken off the line. She didn't have many friends and so it was easy for Thomas to find out if any of her friends knew where she was. He didn't want to look stupid in front them, so he would have to find a clever way of asking about his woman's whereabouts. He set out to do just that.

Day 12

She was wearing an alluring red gown, and Mark couldn't take his eyes off her. He took her to his coach, and when they sat in it, he gave her a beautiful jewel-encrusted box.

"Open it," he said.

She was amazed by the contents. In the box were two velvet pouches. She opened the smaller of the two pouches and in it was a three-strand gold necklace with a large ruby pendant in the middle of the longest strand.

"I hope he isn't falling in love with me!" was her first thought.

It was the amount of money that she saw at the bottom of the box that delighted her the most. With this money, she knew that she could definitely achieve her dream.

She turned to him and hugged him.

"Thank you," she whispered fervently in his ear.

"I want you to think about giving up this trade," Mark said to Daffodil earnestly. A lock of blond hair fell over his eyes giving him a boyish look.

"When I come back from England, I want you to be my woman. Mine and mine alone!"

He continued when Daffodil said nothing: "I'd like you to sever all ties with every other man."

"And your wife?" asked Daffodil.

"Don't worry about my wife," he continued. "My wife will never live here. She hates the weather, the trade and everything about plantation life."

"Ok Mark," she said breathlessly, as she threw her arms around his neck. She explored his ear with the tip of her tongue and sent shivers down his spine.

"I will! I will be your woman!"

Old man Heze Kaya took delivery of everything and had them stored in the caves on the northernmost part of the island a little way away from Francis Bay. Later, he would hand everything over to King Mingo, as planned. Everything was going according to plan. The old man had one problem: he still didn't know how to inform his family about the goings on. He didn't feel the hard calluses on his face as he rubbed his head and his face in despair. He was hoping, that soon, he would find a way.

Day 11

As the large consignment of drinks was delivered to the Pirate's fort, Peegee drew up a roster. Every six hours, four people would be on duty.

"The people on duty today will take the drinks to the ship," he said.

Peegee made sure that everyone knew when they would be on duty, what they would take with them and where they would store them. The operations had to work like clockwork.

"There are to be no mistakes on the days preceding The Major Operation and no mistakes during the takeover of the ship in question."

"Aye! Aye, sir!" was the chorused answer.

The pirates coordinated everything like ants in a colony.

Thomas walked the length and breadth of Coral Bay. None of June Plum's friends seemed to know where she was and he was very worried. Maybe... just maybe, he might meet her coming back home from wherever she might have gone to. Or maybe, he might find some clues to the whereabouts of June Plum. His mind was June Plum so much so, that he was startled when a man stealthily emerged from the bushes. Over the man's shoulders, he carried a large sack. Thomas followed him, wondering where he was going and what he had in the sack. Maybe the man had stolen something. It looked like another arrest might be imminent. He followed at a safe distance observing him. The man stopped at the back door of a house and knocked. A female opened the door. The man didn't enter the house. Rather, he lay the sack on the ground and opened it. He pulled out what looked like a large deer. The woman who had first opened the door, called out to someone inside the house. A little girl came running out. Following behind the little girl, was June Plum!

Day 10

Thomas spent the evening observing Axelina's house. He stood at a safe distance and waited. Maybe June Plum had a new man. If she did, he wanted to know who the upstart was. How could she betray him so badly?

He was surprised when June Plum and Axelina stole out of the house at the stroke of midnight. Thomas followed them without being seen. They didn't speak to each other till they got to the shore where they were greeted by a man in a canoe. Thomas couldn't make the man out. He heard murmurs as they spoke to each other, but he was too far away to hear anything they said. Too bad, he thought. He would wait until they came back. He settled next to a coconut tree and rested his head against the trunk. It might be a long wait, he thought.

It was a few minutes past midnight, when a light easterly wind caused the waves to splash against the sides of the four canoes that bobbed gently on the ocean. The horseshoe shape of the land and the high craggy cliffs shielded them from curious eyes. Once again, only one lantern was lit, and it cast long uneven shadows on the open ocean. So much had gone on, that it seemed as though it was a lifetime since they had last met.

After perfunctory greetings, Kø began.

"We leave on day zero, so we have another ten days to make sure everything is in perfect order. We will meet one more time on day two. And after that, the next time we meet will be on the ship when you hear the sound of the reed."

Everyone took turns to recount what they had done and what was left to be done.

"Don't buy any more ammunition, Boussy," Kø said after Boussy gave his report. "The pirates have delivered enough rounds of cannon and guns on the ship."

Hololegs had made an assortment of small swords like spadroons and rapiers, as well as broadswords, which looked long and deadly, capable of beheading an enemy. He made several bows and arrows as well. The group was impressed by his expertise and the fine samples he presented. Hololegs smiled with pleasure. His broad smile stretched his long face to its absolute limit.

Everyone had done what they were supposed to do, and everything was on course. The countdown was on.

Day 9

Thomas was very angry with himself. He didn't know how he had managed to fall asleep while waiting for June Plum, Axelina and the man who had rowed them out to sea. He thought he should have heard something. He kicked himself in anger.

Daffodil lay on her back and gazed at the ceiling. This was the first time she ever allowed herself to think of a particular time when she lay on her back in this way. She closed her eyes and willed away the images that tormented her, but the images persisted like a bad rash.

Her stepfather was at the center and the periphery of the images. The man she and her mother lived with, had just bought her a new dress, matching shoes and a pretty hat to go with everything. The dress a beautiful rose color with roses stitched all around the hem. She had just turned thirteen, and her breasts were just budding. This was her first grown-up dress, and she felt very elegant. She felt even more grown-up when her stepfather gave her his arm and helped her up and down the stairs of the carriage instead of carrying her up and down as he used to.

A knock on Daffodil's door interrupted her reverie. It was a new customer. One of those that just passed through. He gave her his watch and the little money that he had for an hour or so of pleasure. The watch seemed expensive enough. He didn't look like the kind of person who would last long. She thrust the matters she had been thinking about out of her mind, blotted out the unwashed smells of the man on top of her and thought about the future. As Kø said the other day, no matter how hot a thing is, it will certainly cool down someday. The man cooled down in no time. She added the money he paid her to her ever-growing stash.

Day 8

The gunshots Daffodil heard seemed so real, that even in her sleep, she could taste the tinny tang of gunpowder at the back of her throat. She leaped out of bed, shivering and sleep fled from her eyes. In the end, she gave up, and sat in the well-worn chair beside the window. The old, nondescript curtain that previously shielded the window was used to mop up excess rainwater during the last hurricane, and finally, a new curtain replaced it.

Daffodil moved the dark, heavy, curtain to one side and looked out into the warm, balmy night. She willed her mind to still as she watched the night slowly transform into foggy, grey dusk. But no matter how hard she fought it, her mind went back again and again to that time... when she was thirteen...when her stepfather brought her to his new plantation. Her mind went back to the night he raped her. And the night of the gunshots...

It was late June. The days were blindingly sunny and the nights, warm and pleasant. It was time to harvest sugarcane. Daffodil was wildly excited about the trip from St Croix to St. John. It was her first trip away from home. Her first trip without her mother. Her first trip on a ferry. Her first trip anywhere! It was the first time she was wearing grown-up clothes specially made for her! Her mother had taken her to the seamstress, and the seamstress carefully took their measurements and made a dozen dresses in similar colors for both of them. Robert, Daffodil's stepfather, had paid for everything - the clothes, the shoes, the hats and even the jewelry that matched each dress. Daffodil and her mother danced around the store, beaming with joy.

"I want you to know, that the plantation will belong to you after I'm gone, Dilly," said Robert indulgently.

He always called her Dilly. He thought Daffodil was the most ridiculous name.

"Mother will supervise the harvesting here on this plantation with the help of the two foremen, and I will show you how everything runs on the other Plantation in St. John," he added.

"You have to dress like the lady of the house now," he said smiling.

"You spoil the girl!" said Daffodil's mother as Daffodil admired the feathers in the hats and the detailed bows and ribbons on their dresses.

"But she is my daughter too, Ruth!" Robert answered. "Fathers are supposed to spoil their daughters, are they not?"

Daffodils mother smiled silently thanking God for her good fortune. Good men were hard to come by, and she was blessed to find a man, and a wealthy man at that, who loved her daughter as his own.

It was dark when Daffodil and her stepfather got to the plantation the following day.

"You need to get some rest, Dilly," said her stepfather kissing her forehead. "We're going to have a very busy day tomorrow."

Later that night, Daffodil was somewhere between waking and sleeping when she felt, rather than heard the door of her bedroom open. Someone was on the bed cuddling her. Startled, she gave a frightened start.

"It's only me, Dilly," the voice said.

She recognized her stepfather's voice and relaxed.

"What is it, father?"

"Shhhhh…I came to make sure everything was OK with you, sleep my dear."

He put his hand under the covers and under her dress. Sleepily, she pushed his hand away. His lips were on her nipples and his fingers brought her to orgasm before she understood what was going on. She hid her face away from him embarrassed and confused by the feelings he had just evoked in her. He kissed her lightly on her forehead.

"Sleep well love," he said as he noiselessly shut the door behind him.

The following day, Daffodil hung her head with a deep feeling of shame when she saw her stepfather. He chuckled and held out a beautiful yellow lace dress.

"This is for you," he said. "I want you to wear this dress today, Dilly," he said handing her the dress. It was a pretty, low-cut dress that hugged and accentuated all her slight, still developing, curves.

"You look like a sunflower in that dress!" Robert said. He tied the yellow ribbon to her hair himself. As he lightly stroked the back of her neck, something happened to her nipples. Her stepfather smiled knowingly.

True to his word, Robert taught her everything about the plantation. For the next few weeks, he taught her how to tell when sugarcane was mature and ready for harvesting.

"It takes between ten and twelve months for the canes to mature," he told her. "And they must reach a height of between nine and twelve feet."

He took her to the windmill and the processing house where he showed her how they used wind power to extract cane juice from mature sugar cane stalks. The stalks were washed and chopped into shreds by a series of rotating knives. Huge rollers pressed the juice out of the shredded pulp. He showed her how the freshly squeezed cane juice was fermented and distilled into rum. He taught her how to separate molasses from sugar and even let her taste a little new rum and aged rum, so she could tell the difference.

Daffodil was there when he negotiated for his goods to be sold. She observed all the meticulous details, as he made entries in his logbook, and showed her where he banked his money. He told her to keep the combination to his safe, where he kept all his cash and precious items, secret. They laughed together as they silently mouthed the combination and she swore to keep the secret.

It was past mid-summer before Robert entered Daffodil's room once more. Daffodil thought she had heard a carriage coming in, but she was too tired from the day's work, so she snuggled deeper into her bed. Robert's steps were stealthy, and he was close before she realized he was there.

"Father?" she called.

"Dilly," he answered, sitting on the bed.

He lay beside her, took her face with his hands and kissed her on the cheek.

"You are not only pretty my dear," he said, "you are also very intelligent. I'm so glad you're not my daughter!"

With that, he forced his tongue into her mouth and pinned her under his body.

"I've waited so long for this!" he said into her mouth.

"Noooo!" she cried. "Noooooo!" and broke into a cold sweat.

"Am I not your daughter Papa?" she stammered confused.

He continued his lustful ministrations in earnest.

"Please, please don't!" she cried struggling and pushing him off with her puny strength.

Robert was past the point of no return. He held her down with one arm and swiftly took off her underwear. He covered her cries with his mouth while his fingers found her sensitive spot. He toyed with it till her back began to arch. Swiftly, he entered her and pushed hard against her hymen. Daffodil screamed; she was helpless against the assault. Robert slowed down.

"If you want to ever leave this place alive, Dilly, you will stop screaming!" he told her in an ominous voice.

"And if you want your mother to live, you will never tell her what happened here. If you ever do," he continued, "you will not live to see another day, and neither will she."

With that, Daffodil stilled as hot tears soaked her pillow. Robert leisurely continued what he had started. He was an experienced man, and he knew what he wanted. He took and gave till Daffodil achieved her first real orgasm. He let her go and gathered up his scattered clothes.

"Dilly," he called out to her when he reached the doorway.

The face she lifted up, was a study in confusion, shame and horror. Robert was standing in the doorway, with his arm around a tall, handsome young man. He appeared to be in his early twenties.

"Dilly, this is Mark," he said smiling. "Mark is my god-son. He lives in England and will be with us for the rest of the summer."

None of Robert's words registered and Daffodil looked blankly from one man to the other.

"Mark," he said to the young man, "I have prepared Dilly for you. Once she has cleaned herself up, she is all yours. A young man has to get all the practice he needs before he gets married. She's yours...practice as much as you like!"

And for the next few weeks, Robert schooled Daffodil in the art of sex: and Mark, who was in seventh heaven, happily honed in his sexual skills with her. No matter how much she cried, protested and fought, they took turns and pounded into her aching body until she learned to give the pleasure they sought and take the pleasure they gave.

It was much later, in early fall, that Daffodil's mother, on a hunch that something was amiss, went to the Plantation late one evening, unannounced. There, she found her common-law husband having sex with her only daughter. The sight of his hard, undulating buttocks as he dug into, and prepared to dig once more into her child, sent her beyond the edge of sanity. She screamed her daughter's name in pain and startled them both. As Robert separated himself from her daughter, Daffodil's mother, emptied all five bullets, from his prized 1838 Colt

Patterson revolver, into his body. It was only when she heard a series of futile, empty clicks, that she flung the gun away. Then she held her daughter in her arms and tried to find words of comfort. She found none. Through her tears, her mother saw that Daffodil's eyes were no longer the eyes of a child. Daffodil had gone past childhood, scaled over adolescence and settled in a place where she, her mother, would never fully understand. In a few short months, her daughter had stopped crying the willful tears of a child. She had suddenly grown up to become a woman whose eyes had become hard, knowing and timeless.

Day 7

June Plum unceremoniously broke off her relationship with her man. She cut him off cleanly...like a hot knife cutting through the butter that she and Axelina had just churned. She didn't have time to sit and whine about anything. She was too busy. Her man loved many women and had several children with different women. He loved her not only for her ample proportions (as he put it, he liked his women juicy, as juicy as a june plum!) but also because she was easy going and accommodated his occasional indiscretions.

Her man loved his children much more than he loved his women and June Plum knew that there was no way he would want to leave the island and leave his children behind. Besides, he had what he considered to be a good job with the law. Indeed, he was **The Law** in St John. There was no way she was going to tell him about their plans. The only thing was, she didn't know how to break up with him. She decided to make herself scarce.

"Out of sight, out of mind," she thought to herself. "If he can't find me, he'll get the message."

The *kitchen bitch* was not allowed to go out in Axelina's kitchen. It gave off poor light and noxious fumes, but from sundown to sunup, Axelina and June Plum were tireless as they cooked up a storm. They stored the beef jerky and all the other salted and dried foods in the new wooden drums that Kø had made with Shippy's help. Some of the drums were filled with salt pork and others filled with salt fish. The starches were dried and pounded into coarse or fine powder. The corn was pounded into corn meal. Fruits and vegetables were still drying out, and other fruits were stewed, juiced and candied. There was no time for June Plum to think about or dwell on heartbreak.

Day 6

Daffodil was still in a pensive mood when she met Mark at the Tavern. He had never seen her like that and he was most concerned. Daffodil was astonished that he didn't recognize her. Yes, those terrible events happened nine years ago. But had she changed so much? The fact that he didn't recognize her, showed her just how insignificant she had been then, and she still was. She was just a sexual toy to him. He didn't think her thoughts and feelings mattered. To him and his godfather, she was just a vessel to be used and thrown away. Mark would realize soon enough just how inconvenient life could be when he paid for his and his godfather's sins with everything he owned. She allowed two drops of tears to run down her cheeks. Then she wiped the rest of the tears angrily with the back of her hand, swallowed the memories with a large gulp, thrust out her chin and focused on the tasks ahead.

Day 5

All day, there was a chaotic hive of activity at the Pirates' fort, but it was a strategically organized chaos. Each man knew just what to do, and they busily unloaded, counted and repacked boxes in the courtyard. They stacked the boxes from floor to ceiling. They contained all sort of things the pirates felt they needed. Food, drinks, ammunition and even musical instruments. Peegee paced up and down the long rectangular room. In seven days, the Spanish ship, *La Vitória,* would be within pillaging sight. The cargo was meant for the Spanish Monarchy, and it was soon going to belong to him and his men. He went over the plan again in his mind. The plan was flawless. He made sure all the gang rehearsed everything until they knew what to do in their sleep. He had been a pirate for more than two decades and he intended to enjoy the final fruits of his labor. This "labor" was for his retirement. It would provide him with everything a man could ever want till his dying day. He intended to die a rich man with a woman like Daffodil by his side. He gave himself a small smile as he thought about the money, precious stones and medicines on board. Medicines always fetched a huge premium. His heart raced in excitement as he watched his men prepare to load the ship again once darkness fell.

After everything was in place, he intended to visit Daffodil. He could feel the tension in his back and knew just what to do to ease it up. He hadn't been with Daffodil for a while, and he badly needed that woman! He thought about all the things she did to him with her small, adept fingers and slowly, his face lost its fierce concentration and finally gave in to a broad winsome smile.

Axelina and June plum exchanged perplexed looks when they heard the knock on the door just shy of midnight. It wasn't the coded knock they came to expect. The knock came again and again growing louder till it became a loud continuous banging.

"I know you're in there, June Plum!" Thomas shouted, "Open this door!"

June Plum and Axelina looked at each other in consternation. The banging grew louder and stopped as suddenly as it started.

"I give you three seconds, June Plum," Thomas said loudly, "And then I will break down this door down if I have to."

June Plum looked at Axelina and shrugged helplessly as she opened the door. Thomas stood there, his muscles taught and strained, his face dark and angry, like the roiling clouds before a storm. He grabbed her hand unceremoniously and dragged her all the way to her house. He sat her down on the bed they had shared so many times together.

"You have to tell me what the matter is, June Plum. You have to tell me why you have decided to throw our relationship away just like that. I have a right to know, and you have to tell me tonight!"

"There is nothing the matter," June Plum insisted "I just don't want to continue with our relationship anymore."

"That can't be true! Thomas retorted, "Give me a reason why. I want to know why."

"Thomas," June Plum said angrily, "Just leave me alone!"

Thomas held her and looked into her eyes. "It must be another man isn't it? The man who brought the deer to Axelina's house that day?"

He stroked the back of her neck with light tender strokes.

"Why won't you accept that it's over between us, Thomas? It's over I say!"

"If you say so my love." He said. "For old times' sake can I have one last hug? At least you can give me that!"

Thomas turned to her and hugged her hard. He stoked the back of her neck again. That was her most sensitive spot and he knew it. He planted little kisses on the side of her neck and when he tongued her ear, and rubbed his hands lightly over her, June Plum sighed with pleasure. Thomas undressed her in record time. He took his time to explore every inch of her ample proportions. Before long, June Plum was a quivering mass of pudding, as they rolled around her bed.

Day 4

June Plum was totally naked and fast asleep when Thomas woke up just before dawn. He smiled at her light snoring, and then, frowned with concern. He couldn't understand June Plum's reticence. He couldn't make sense of her behavior. There was something going on and he would get to the bottom of it, if it was the last thing he did.

He took careful aim at the nipple closest to him and wrapped his warm lips around it. His fingers carefully parted her thighs till he found what he was looking for. He teased it lightly. June Plum was bucking her hips wildly before she was fully awake.

"Now Thomas!" she begged, "now!"

"Not until you tell me what is going on...."

"I can't!"

Thomas stilled. She writhed under him.

"Please!"

"Just tell me," he coaxed.

"Nooooo!"

"Tell me," he crooned into her ear, "I won't be angry, I just want to understand you."

"Nooooo!"

June Plums whimpering turned into frustrated crying.

"It was all Ko's idea," she cried, "we are going steal a ship and go to Africa!"

"And you were going without me?" he asked planting gentle kisses on the side of her neck, "You can't go without me June Plum. I won't let you!"

"You can't stop me Thomas!" she retorted.

Thomas kissed her fiercely, drowned out her protests and gave her the best loving she had ever had.

Axelina clutched at Mandy's hand firmly as together they trotted over to Kø's little house. She had waited all night for June Plum to come back and when she hadn't, Axelina was most concerned. Seeing how determined Thomas was when he almost broke down her door, she knew there was going to be trouble. She just knew it! She was panting when she finally got to Kø's home. She knocked hard at the door several times. There was no answer. He might be at Daffodils or Boussy's or Hololegs home. She went to each person's home. No-one was home. That wasn't surprising, everyone was busy getting things ready.

The shop keeper's assistant wasn't pleased to see Daffodil. His master didn't like 'those types' near his establishment, and neither did he. They were bad for business. But when Daffodil opened her palm and showed him her money, he turned a blind eye to her profession and sold her the two kegs of premium imported beer she asked for.

"Can you have them delivered to me in two days?" she asked putting extra money for delivery on his table.

The shop keeper's assistant's bulbous nose twitched with pleasure. Daffodil had paid him far more than was necessary for delivery and he slyly pocketed the extra money.

When the beer was delivered to her two days later, Daffodil opened both kegs and put in a muslin bag of carefully selected herbs. The herbs had to steep overnight to be effective. In the morning, she would remove the muslin bag and have the kegs delivered to Captain Peegee and his cronies up at his fort.

Up in the hills, from their vantage point, King Mingo and a group of twenty men were watching the ship. Almost two hundred Maroons were at the beach, safely hidden in various caves. They were under strict orders not to come out till they were instructed to do so. There was to be no noise and no evidence of their existence. King Mingo brooked no nonsense, and they knew him well enough not to disobey any of his orders.

The canoes that would cart people and produce were ready, hidden among the reed brushes not too far away. In two days, they would pack everything onto the canoes, and transport themselves and their booty to Africa via Denmark as planned.

Day 3

A group of King Mingo's men settled up in the trees that surrounded the pirates' fort. They camouflaged themselves with leaves and twigs and sat perfectly still. Only their eyes moved to and fro, as they carefully watched the goings on in the Peegee's fort. They wanted no surprises.

No-one asked where he found it, but one of King Mingo's sons, Lyon, produced a pair of binocular instruments, and they took turns in observing the ship, its occupants and the goings on in the environs. Kø had given them all the information about the ship's activities, and they knew what to do and what to expect. They had only one chance to do things right, and they intended to make no mistakes. Tomorrow, they would move in and seize the ship.

"The upstart!" Thomas thought to himself, he was going to have to deal with Kø himself. He couldn't arrest him because he hadn't broken the law. This was a personal matter and he would have to deal with it personally. He checked the rapier hidden under his shirt. It was there, sharp and ready to separate flesh from bone. His gun was already loaded. "Africa, my foot!" He thought angrily. That African man was going to be a dead and buried by the morning.

For once, Kø was tired. The activities at the fort were getting more and more hectic and the activities he had to coordinate with Boussy, King Mingo and the others before they left, were even more intense. But he couldn't rest until they were on their way to Denmark.

The mountain road was dark and lonely and the night, still. He thought he heard something unusual, but he wasn't sure. He plodded along thinking about all their plans. Suddenly, a figure jumped out of the bushes, into his line of vision.

"So you intend to take my woman with you to Africa, do you?" the voice asked.

"Wha…what?" he stammered.

"I know all about your plans!" said Thomas seething.

"What?"

"June Plum told me everything…What makes you think you can come here, disrupt our lives and take our women away huh?"

Kø doubled over in pain when a fist landed in his stomach. As soon as he straightened up, another landed on his face. Vicious blows were rained on him as the man spoke in deep grunts.

"You can swim the ocean back to Africa, but you're not taking my woman," he swore, "and you're not taking my people!"

Kø tried to back-pedal, to get away from the hail of punches Thomas rained on him. The man's punches stung like bee stings and Kø could feel his eye begin to shut and his face begin to swell. Thomas was as tall as Kø, but was heavier and more muscular. Kø wrapped him in a fierce clinch to stop the blows. Thomas disengaged and pushed him away. Kø staggered backwards.

A sudden movement caught King Mingo's son Lyon's eye as he scanned his environs through his binocular instrument. It was dark, and he wasn't sure what the movement was. He looked again. There it was! The movement he thought he saw. Two men were fighting. The hair looked familiar. He took a closer look.

Thomas eyes were red, glazed, and intent on one thing. He bared his teeth and Kø realized that this was a fight to the death. Kø faked a punch to disorient his opponent. His opponent moved in the direction he wanted him to move. With all his might, Kø punched Thomas in the jaw. Thomas brain rattled in his head. He saw stars and fell to the ground.

Lyon, descended from his perch in the trees in record time, grabbed his brother and another man by the arm and together, they started running.

"What's going on?" the others asked.

"You, come with me!" he said urgently handing over the binocular instrument to another man as his brother and friend followed hard on his heels.

"And you stay!"

Kø bent over Thomas to feel his pulse. He was still breathing. He figured he would have to find a way of getting Thomas out of the way till they were aboard that ship. He felt himself for any broken bones. Fortunately for him, apart from bruises, a black eye and a broken nose, he was alright. He wiped his bloody nose on his sleeve.

Thomas came round quickly and felt for his gun. He aimed at Kø's head and fired. Kø fell to the ground. King Mingo's sons, Lyon and Tigga, leaped upon Thomas. They struggled to take the gun away while their friend knelt down to see if Kø was still alive. Thomas fired at Kø one more time. The bullet hit the kneeling man in the back. The man slumped over. Lyon finally over-powered Thomas. His brother snatched the gun out of

Thomas' hand, turned the gun on him and fired. The bullet blew a hole where Thomas's right eye used to be.

Day 2

Daffodil was thinking about getting someone to deliver the keg of beer to Peegee's fort when a loud banging disturbed her tranquil evening. She gave a startled jump. It couldn't be Mark; he never came to her home. Maybe it was Kø. She hurriedly dumped the clothes she was packing into a trunk and moved the trunk out of the way. She opened the door when the person started pounding away at it again, and Peegee almost fell into the room.

Her eyes registered her surprise.

"I know, I know!" he said to Daffodil. "But I just had to see you today."

She gave a little frown. He reached into his pocket and brought out a wad of notes. He was always very generous to her, and she needed the money now more than ever. She felt the wad. It was hard and substantial in her hands, and she deliberately changed her mood.

"In fact, I was just thinking about you. I hadn't seen you in so long and I thought you had abandoned me!" she said smiling at him.

Peegee needed no other invitation; he fell onto Daffodil like a half-starved animal. He tore off her clothes and had his way with her, right there, where she stood! He pummeled her when she was underneath him, on top of him and every way he could think of. And after she had rested sufficiently from the first round of his affectionate ministrations, he started all over again till his substantial lustful appetite was finally sated.

"I was going to have those delivered to you because I missed you!" Daffodil said wearily, pointing at the kegs.

"I heard the beer had just been imported and I thought you would like to try it."

He grinned and hefted both kegs under his arms. Now that he was satisfied, he would enjoy the beer with the men when he got back to the Fort. This would be their very last drink, and then they would "dry out" before the "operation."

Day 1

Darkness covered the sea, and deep, dark clouds covered the heavens. Four boats seemed to float aimlessly on the ocean. They couldn't be the canoes of fishermen because no one seemed to be in the boats. The men lay inside the canoes waiting. At the thin, shrill sound of the reed pipe, eight muscled men neatly cut into the sea, hardly making a sound. The canoes were not anchored. They let them float out to the open sea. Their muscles rippled as they swam silently toward the ship. Strapped to their chests, were a variety of dangerous looking daggers, rapiers and spadroons. And strapped to their backs were bows and several arrows. They carried no guns. They had no intention of attracting any attention. They circled the ship till they heard the sound of the reed pipe playing a familiar tune. They swam in the direction of the sound and found a rope ladder. Soft-footed, they climbed and landed on the deck. The man with the reed flute continued to play his instrument. The eight men stealthily spread out. Not for a minute did they take their eyes off of the three pirates.

Three of the eight men knelt and took aim with their bows and arrows. The music from the reed pipe continued to play. They swiftly released their arrows. Two of the men were struck in the heart. One arrow sailed right past the third man standing at the bow of the ship. He didn't know what sped past his head, and he turned to see what it was. He couldn't make it out. He turned to survey the direction the thing came from. A man with a deadly looking dagger flicked his wrist. The man turned just in time to receive the dagger in his forehead. He staggered backward and fell overboard. The music stopped. The two dead men were thrown overboard. All evidence of their demise was erased. The eight men took position. Kø inspected his reed pipe through his good eye. The other eye was still swollen shut. Fortunately for him, because of Lyon's intervention, Thomas's bullet caused a superficial wound when it grazed his shoulder. He pushed pain into the recesses of his being, took his position at the lookout and waited patiently for the next group of men who would come to relieve him. Their fates were sealed.

Deep in the caves, the Maroon women, their children, the aged and the rest of the men who weren't out on special duty were busy. They wouldn't rest till every canoe was packed and ready to sail. Silently, they loaded every canoe with wooden barrels, sacks, and wooden trunks. It was almost time!

Day 0

It looked as though a tree moved, but Johnny, the guard, wasn't sure. It was very dark out there, and the moon refused to give off any light. What Johnny was sure about though, was that he was tired, and he wished he could have some sleep. He yawned widely. It was the sort of yawn that stretched one's face to the limit and went on and on for a while and refused to subside. The yawn brought tears to his eyes, and he wiped the tears tiredly.

He shut his eyes for a few seconds just to rest them. The seconds turned to minutes…

The trees moved closer to the house. Their leaves rustled in the wind. Johnny's head nodded sharply. When he peeled open his bleary eyes, a tree was standing right in front of him. Out of the tree trunk, black eyes stared at him. Johnny rubbed his eyes. Maybe he was in dreamland. Another tree moved to his left. Johnny shut his eyes tightly, rubbed them with his fists and opened them again. Several pairs of sinister black eyes stared out at him from the tree trunks. He opened his mouth to shout. But a knife from nowhere, pierced him in the stomach. He groaned. The tree angled the knife at a one hundred-eighty degree angle to do major damage to Johnny's internal organs. Johnny opened his eyes widely in double surprise just before the tip of the knife sliced his heart. The tree trunk that held him laid him down gently behind some bushes and his closed surprised eyes. Other trees moved closer.

Earlier, rain had cooled the night air. Mark and his household were fast asleep. With the guard taken care of, several trees entered the servant's rooms and bound them hand and foot.

Daffodil had done a great job of showing them where everything was. She had drawn them a map with all the details they needed, so everything was easy to identify. They entered Mark's room easily and found him sprawled, snoring, fully clothed, across his bed. A half-empty bottle of rum and an empty glass stood on the side table beside his bed. Five men simultaneously blindfolded him, bound his mouth, spread-eagled him and tied his hands and feet to his four-poster bed before he properly awoke. They took the remains of the rum and the glass he was drinking from and put it in a sack. Then, methodically and systematically they ransacked the plantation according to Daffodil's instructions. They first took the safe from its hiding place. Daffodil would figure out how to open it later. Then they packed up every moveable item – clothing, jewelry, and money. They packed pots, pans, and crockery, furniture, food and more. As swiftly and as silently as they entered, they hauled every portable item and left.

The fort was quiet. Peegee and his men were enjoying a deep, drug-induced sleep. Their mouths were slack, and the mugs that had held fresh, crisp, imported beer had fallen out of their limp fingers.

Up in the trees that surrounded the fort, a dozen men sat like panthers camouflaged by leaves. Their eyes were alert, their muscles taut. They were armed to the teeth. Just in case any of the pirates woke up, they would make sure that they wouldn't live to sound an alarm. Their canoes were well hidden in a cove nearby. As soon as they saw the flag **Metrova** hoisted, they would be on their way to board the ship. They settled on the branches, slowed their breath and counted down to freedom.

The night was still and waiting. Those who were going to travel had been sitting on tenterhooks all day, waiting for the sound from the reed. When the sound came, it was thin and shrill and went on at sporadic intervals. After the seventh sound, Boussy smiled and stood up. He stretched his stocky self to full height. He flexed his muscles and thrust his chin forward. Short as he was, he looked like a commander in an army.

"This," Boussy said to his friends, "is the real sound of freedom! Not freedom that I have been given, but the freedom that I have decided to take for myself. It is not a decision that has been made for me, but one that I have made for myself!"

There were others who had been kidnapped like Boussy, and others who chose to come with them. Their faces shone with excitement. The group of thirty-five people left in batches of twos and threes at different intervals so as not to attract attention. They headed for the caves where King Mingo and the other Maroons waited with all their belongings. All the canoes were ready, and the oarsmen were ready to row them to the ship. The ship was secured with two dozen fully armed Maroons already stationed on it. Everything they needed, and more, was in place. No-one looked back when they left Boussy's little shanty.

Axelina and her daughter, Mandy, went to fetch Old Man Heze Kaya from his house. His small house was filled with happy sounds: Two of his sons, who had been sold to other plantations, had managed to find their way back to him, and they were there with their wives, children and grandchildren. The old man didn't know how to leave. He looked at Axelina with sad eyes and gave a slight shake of his head. He just couldn't leave them ... not now. This was his family. His heart was here, on this island, in this room. Time had planted him too firmly on the island and time had torn up any roots he had with the African continent. The ocean between him and Africa was too vast. The ties he had now were too strong, too deep, too tangled and too emotional to break. Axelina gave a small nod of understanding. Her heart was heavy for him, but there was no time to waste.

June Plum had not come back home since the day Thomas came knocking. Axelina supposed she had decided to reconcile with him. June Plum *should* have told her if she had changed her mind.

The reed sounded again and she, her daughter left in the horse-drawn cart.

Shippy hopped onto the back of Axelina's cart. He lay his cutlass on the bed of the cart and fingered the dagger under his belt. Satisfied, he turned his thoughts elsewhere. His thoughts were full of hope. Maybe a woman in Africa would accept him for who he was - a one-armed man. Maybe he could also have a wife of his own, have children and grow old with them. Then he did something he had hardly ever done because he was so ashamed of his disability. ...he lifted his head and held it high. Maybe, he thought to himself, just maybe, life might be better when he went back home to Africa. He smiled, and his handsome face was transformed.

Ezekiel had delivered the sails, rope, paint and the new flag with *The Metrova* painted on it. Everything was already aboard, and he would help Kø and the others hoist the sails and lift the anchor once everyone was safely aboard. Kø didn't want to hoist things too soon just in case a pirate or someone discovered what was going on. He pocketed his well-thumbed Bible and hymn book and, humming his favorite tune, he walked out of the door at the sound of the reed flute. His knife was in his other pocket, and his gun was safely hidden under his shirt.

Because of Thomas' attack on Kø, a group of twenty-five men were stationed on different parts of the island to make sure there would be no surprise attacks. Hololegs and Hunter were chosen to supervise them. The group of about twenty-five were to board the ship after everyone was safely on board.

Part 5

"You

will never know

the importance of buttocks

until

they develop a boil!"

African proverb

24

Daffodil stepped out of Kø's house, and he followed closely behind her. His black eye was getting better, but nose was crooked and his face still puffy and tender from the beating Thomas had given him. Daffodil had cleaned the bullet wound. Thankfully it was superficial. It throbbed painfully but he couldn't afford to dwell on that pain. The hour had come. He had to finish what he had started.

Kø had a new respect for Daffodil's boldness, bravery and meticulous planning. First, she had saved his life twice. Then the money she had shared with him would be enough for anything he wanted to do in Denmark and back home in Africa. Her painstaking planning and foresight amazed him!

Daffodil had sent a few kegs of newly brewed imported beer, which she laced with valerian root, passion flower, kava and senna leaves to Peegee. It would be at least nine hours before the Pirates could wake up. And when they finally woke up, they would be hopping from foot to foot, looking for the nearest lavatory. By that time, they would far away. For once in a very long time, Kø smiled his lopsided smile.

Daffodil looked to the future. She knew how to get what she wanted, and she was going to buy that inn and be an innkeeper. It didn't matter that they couldn't go to Port Royal in Jamaica, which used to be the richest place in the world. That was where she really wanted to buy her inn. However, word had it that the city had sunk due to an earthquake, so she decided to go to Quitta with Kø. There were still merchants trading on the coast and visitors would always need a place to stay. She felt for her money, and her precious gems...most of them were tied in small pouches firmly secured to a string which she tied around her waist. The skirt she wore was voluminous enough to hide any trace of her fortune. The money Mark had given her made her stash heavier but who was she to complain? Besides, the less she thought about Mark, the better. He, like his uncle, had just used her. She made them pay for what they did to her. Daffodil allowed herself a small, mischievous smile.

She felt for Kø's uninjured hand and looked at this tall, gentleman who had become like a brother to her. He was now her only family, and she liked the idea of having a capable big brother. Finally, she belonged.

"You never told me the meaning of your name, Kø," Daffodil said suddenly, as they walked away from her house.

She trod carefully avoiding the large rocks strewn along the path.

"The name Kondo? My mother named me after a warrior," Kø answered, giving her a sideways glance.

"But why did she name you after a warrior?"

"She told my father when I was born, that I would have to straddle both Africa and Europe, and overcome the limitations and prejudices of both continents. She said to function comfortably wherever I chose to live, I would have to have the heart of a warrior!"

"Ah, that makes a lot of sense!" she said. "Because that's just who you are! I'm sure your mother never imagined that you would ever find yourself in this part of the world!"

Together, in companionable silence, they walked to the shore at Drunk Bay, climbed into the waiting canoe and sailed round the East End of the island straight to the ship.

At the fort, the men began to wake one by one. Not only did they have a terrible hangover from drinking too much, but the effects of the long hours of sleep also left them slightly disoriented. No sooner had they woken up, than the men started to fight their way to the few lavatories in the fort.

The men in the trees were satisfied with the chaos going on in the fort. They silently climbed down from their perches and swiftly made their way to *The Metrova*.

Thomas's colleagues at the Police Station were desperately looking for him. In the seven or so years that he worked as a policeman, he had never been absent from work - not even when he was unwell. When they found his home vacant, they checked June Plum's home. They found her bed rumpled and a meal half eaten. A search party was dispatched to look for both of them. The search party was under strict orders to check every house, every mountain and every valley for the love birds. June Plum's body turned up in the abandoned sugar plantation, with the rope that snuffed her life out, still tight around her neck. The search party dreaded to think about the whereabouts of Thomas.

When Pirate Peegee found out that the sailors who were on duty that night did not come back to the Fort, he wondered what had happened to them and what had happened to the batch that had gone out to relieve them. He took his binocular telescope and looked out in the direction of the ship. In the horizon was a strangely similar ship. The sails were new, the flag was different, and the name was different! Even the paint on the sides of the ship was different. He swung his binocular telescope this way and that way, scanning the horizon. There were no other ships anywhere in the distance! There seemed to be quite a bit of activity on the ship. Little canoes, laden with people sailed towards the ship. Awareness suddenly hit him like a bullet shot at close range. The contents of his stomach threatened to gush out from all orifices of his body. He rushed to the top of the cliff with guns blazing, shooting into the air. His red hair stood on end like a crazy, raging brushfire. He fired shots into the air several times, screaming with rage. Those who could come to his aid were either too groggy to move or holding their stomachs and backsides, desperately trying to find an unoccupied lavatory. Peegee ran back to the fort, got a cache of guns and bullets. He forced some of his colleagues at gun point to help him and ready some boats. He didn't care that some of them were still in their nightshirts. A war was on!

Meanwhile, almost everyone was on *The Metrova*. They were waiting for Hololegs, Hunter, and the last two or three canoes to arrive. A young man, one of the eight who initially secured the ship, was perched on the top-most mast. His job was to alert Kø and the crew if there was any unusual activity. A series of gunshots rang out, and the man on the lookout fell from his eighty foot perch, and his body spattered onto the deck. Boussy ran out to see what was happening. He was met with gunshots as Peegee and his men gained in on the ship.

"Kø!" he cried, "We have to lift up anchor NOW ! Peegee and his men are gaining in on us!"

"Is everyone aboard?" Kø asked, thinking of Hololegs, Hunter and the rest.

"No, but we don't have a moment to loose!" Boussy cried.

Kø sprang into action.

"You!" He gave orders to a group of men and women who had been trained to shoot, "get to the cannon! Fire!"

"You, get more guns! Keep them at bay! Shoot to kill!"

"You, lift up anchor! **NOW!**"

Hololegs and the men in the boats rowed as quickly as possible. They lowered their heads to avoid the hail of bullets raining on them. All three boats got to the rope ladder at almost the same time. A bullet hit the man next to Hololegs. He let out a hi-pitched squeal and fell into the water. Hololegs and a few of the men dived into the water. The boat was no longer safe. Bullets hit the surface of the water and smashed open any heads that bobbed on the surface. Shots were exchanged as Kø's men took aim at the Pirate's boats. The waves churned blood and water. Other men desperately struggled to climb up the rope ladder to get onto the Metrova. In their desperation, they pulled each other down. The ship heaved forward. Those who attempted to climb, flailed helplessly as the ship began to move and fell into the sea. When the gunfire finally ceased, armed men and women stood guard all around the deck of the Metrova. They stood there and took no rest until the dawn broke.

When the Island of was not even a speck in the distance, Ezekiel sank to his knees and raised his arms to God for such an awesome deliverance! Every man, woman and child dropped to their knees as Ezekiel prayed. The joy that they would have felt, was tempered by the loss of friends, lovers and partners in the get-away plan. They lost about thirty men including Hololegs and Hunter.

"Freedom never comes easy," said King Mingo to the mournful crowd, "It has to be demanded and fought for. There is always a price to pay. This is the price we had to pay."

And as they sailed north, they resolved to put the past behind them. Kø had carved out a fearsome African warrior out of mahogany, which he nailed to the bow. He decorated the stern with a huge carving of a dolphin. The pirates had loaded the ship with many guns and ammunition, food and drinks. Besides that, there was so much loot from the Greenville Plantation that Kø and his new kinsmen had excess of everything. It was indeed a wealthy ship that sailed away from the West Indies that day.

Part 6

Though the earth is solid,

the chameleon

treads gently.

Ewe Proverb

25

The temporary euphoria after the 'great escape' did not last long. As Kø faced the Northern Star and maneuvered his ship towards Denmark, he wondered how he was going to face his father, General Sønne and those who condoned his demise.

"I really don't see why you want to see your father," Daffodil said one day, "I grew up without a father and I'm fine!"

"I thought about it as well," said King Mingo "And do you trust these white men? Look at what they tried to do to you!"

"It's not about color." Boussy retorted, "It's about relationship! I had a close relationship with my father as well, so I know how Kø feels."

"Well," said King Mingo, "whatever happens Kø, know that we are your family now."

"Thank you, my friends. Thank you."

"You know, you shouldn't just barge into your father's house immediately we get to Copenhagen," said King Mingo.

The room was quiet when Daffodil asked. "How do you know if he will accept you?"

"He will!" Kø said stubbornly. "He has to!"

"What about your enemies?" asked Boussy. "Do you know what they will do to you if they find out you're in their country? You could be in real danger!"

"You always said we should have a plan and work the plan," interjected Daffodil "We are going to have to have a very good plan!

"Indeed, we have to craft a *great* plan before you go into Copenhagen!" Boussy agreed.

Kø sat down heavily in the chair. He looked at his closest friends. They were his new family. He saw the concern on their faces, and he knew they were right.

"I think I should be the one to go into the city to find out about your family and your enemies." Daffodil said suddenly.

"You?" The men exclaimed. "A *woman*? This is dangerous work you know!"

"Think about it." Daffodil said calmly. "I, *a woman*, am the best person to go into Copenhagen. I can find out everything about the Quist family, General Sønne and Captain Laarsen. I will be the least conspicuous and the most effective."

The men looked at her with new admiration. Their admiration was not lost on her and she smiled.

263

"But you can't go alone" said Kø. "I couldn't live with myself if something were to happen to you. You must go with some body- guards."

"Bodyguards?" cried Daffodil. "No, that won't work at all! We will be too conspicuous, and they will arouse too much curiosity! "I will go by myself." She said. "I can shoot and use that dagger well as well. I will be fine!"

"What if the bodyguards who went with you were dressed as women?" King Mingo asked. He was always the master of camouflage.

They all burst into laughter. Quickly, they identified three handsome youths on the ship. They had been born to white plantation owners, and they could wield a dagger and shoot as well as any man. Indeed, they could slit a throat if they had to. They would make perfect 'ladies'!

"Ezekiel!!!!" Kø shouted as he opened the door. "You have women's clothes to make!"

26

Spring, 1853

Spring had just begun when they finally berthed just outside the territorial waters of Denmark a few months later. It was one of those days that nature assured you that it would be generous with warmth as it had been with cold during the past winter.

The summer sun waltzed over the waters took its own sweet time to set. When it set, and was well below the horizon, it cast a soft glowing light that painted the sky in dramatic shades of blue, grey, orange and pale. By the time Daffodil emerged from her cabin looking like a lady of considerable means, it was twilight. She looked like a rare, beautiful and exotic creature in an emerald green gown.

Daffodil's gown was off the shoulder, showing off her olive skin and rounded shoulders. The blouse, tapered to her waist, emphasized her tiny waist. She wore a large hoop under the skirt that showed off a myriad of tiny flounces, bows and ribbons in varying shades of green. Emeralds, purloined from Mark's plantation, dangled at her ears, nestled between her breasts, and jingled at both wrists. Her dark hair was arranged in a demure bun. At the bottom of the dainty matching handbag, she carried a small, deadly looking dagger, a smorgasbord of assorted things which she believed she should always carry, and enough money for a week or so.

Ezekiel had altered the clothes for Daffodil's bodyguards very well. The three youths who were to accompany Daffodil ashore were dressed in the most modern of women's clothing and jewelry that had also been filched from the Greenville Estate. Their fashionable hats shielded their faces as they walked daintily to the boats that would take them ashore. Inside their boots were daggers and inside their dainty looking purses where loaded pistols with extra bullets, just in case. Four of King Mingo's men rowed them to the shore, and they were under strict instructions to wait for them no matter how long it took.

When they finally touched the shore just off Copenhagen harbor, Daffodil surreptitiously studied the various coachmen who were vying for her business before she finally settled on a young, dark haired coachman. He was not unattractive; it just seemed that something was somewhat misaligned in his face. As she observed him closely, she saw that his shoulders were curved in a strange way. 'Ah!' she thought to herself, 'Perfect! Perrrrfect!! He's a hunchback!'

The coachman quietly stood in the back and fixed his eyes on her. He had never seen a more beautiful woman, and he silently wished she would choose his services. He had a bad stutter and didn't speak much, but Daffodil could see the longing and admiration in his eyes. She pinned him with her alluring eyes, and he was like a helpless butterfly that had been pinned to the wall. He was helpless, flailing and waiting for her command.

"How much will you charge to take us to Østerbro, Sir?" Daffodil smiled sweetly, climbing into the coach before he answered.

The main street which Magnus, the coachman, drove through was vibrant and people sat and drank coffee or *aqvavit* all_day, while others went from shop to shop looking for deals. It was the perfect place to mingle, to be seen and to get lost in the crowd.

The coach driver bowed deeply when Daffodil tipped him generously as he dropped them off at a boarding house at the end of Main Street.

"Please pick me up in an hour," she said. "I need to go to Valby once we have settled in."

Magnus crumpled his cap in his hand. He couldn't believe his good fortune. She chose him! And she wanted his services again! Wherever Daffodil wanted to go, he would take her. He was ready to wait patiently to take her wherever she wanted.

"D..d..don't worry mmma'aam," Magnus stuttered, "I I I I'll wait for you!"

"We shall not allow you to go alone!" said one of the Daffodil's bodyguards once they settled in their room at the boarding house.

"You have to let me go alone!" she cried.

"But why?" they asked puzzled.

"Because I want as much information as I can from Magnus. If you go with us, he will be tongue-tied, and I need him to relax and give me all the information I need."

There was a lot of argument about Daffodil's insistence on going alone.

"Why do you think I chose a hunchback as a coachman?" she asked them.

"Yes," they queried. "Why did you?"

"You," Daffodil waved a hand that included all of them "of all people should understand what it's like not to be accepted. And so, you should also know what it feels like to be wholly accepted! I understand Magnus' need for genuine acceptance. I have accepted him, and he knows it. And because of that, I have his trust!"

Daffodil was exasperated that they couldn't see things the way she did. After much grumbling, it was finally agreed that Daffodil would go alone. They made sure she was armed to the teeth. The plan was simple. She would locate Kø's father's home, find out as much as possible from Magnus and come right back.

Magnus proved to be an invaluable guide to Daffodil. Because he was a coachman, many people had conversations in his coach which he overheard but never commented on. And because he was a hunchback, many people merely looked at him but didn't really see him. Magnus was an expert at fading into the background, while listening intently to and observing everything. He had heard about the Quist family, and he had much information about them and their dealings. His invaluable information made Daffodil's quest so much easier. He took Daffodil to Valby, to the Quist's address, and Daffodil looked in awe at the grand mansions as they drove past. Kø's father's mansion was on a quiet street of *Smedestræde* not far from the

Søerne. Most of the houses were less than fifteen years old, and according to Magnus, the houses were built and inhabited mostly by successful merchants who had gone to Africa or The Far East to trade. Most of the houses were grand three-storey mansions.

Hans Quist's house was one of these. It had six Grecian columns in front of it, and each of the dozen or so windows was framed on the outside with white plaster of Paris figurines. Heavy velvet curtains shielded the inside from inquisitive, prying eyes. On top of the high red roof were two chimneys. In between the two chimneys were several figurines of beatific angels and ugly gargoyles that grinned malevolently at the scenes that took place in the street.

The wheels of the carriage clattered over the cobbled stones as Magnus turned the carriage round and headed back to *Østerbro.* They traveled in silence for a while, and Daffodil took in the night sights. They went past the bright lanterns of the Tivoli Gardens, and Daffodil wished she could visit the gardens if she ever had a chance.

"I need your help, Magnus," said Daffodil earnestly, fixing her eyes on him. "And I will pay you if you help me."

She opened her bag and took out a wad of notes. Magnus ogled at the money.

"It must be important to you to find these people!"

"It is!" responded Daffodil with a small smile. "It really is!"

"Will you help me?" she asked.

"I will, Daffodil," he answered.

"I need to find out about everyone in the Quist family, General Sønne and his wife Katie and Captain Laarsen."

Daffodil divided the wad of notes into three parts and gave him the third. Magnus couldn't believe his good fortune!

"I want to know all about them," she said. "I want to know where they live, what they do, where they go, what their habits are...everything!"

"We will need your assistance in another way, Magnus," she continued, "and I will give you this other wad once we finish doing everything we came here to do."

It was not till the evening of the fourth day that Magnus finally got all the information Daffodil wanted.

"We need to leave immediately!" Daffodil said to her 'bodyguards.' We don't have a minute to waste!" She paid Magnus, and he promised to wait till they came back so he could assist with whatever else needed to be done.

King Mingo's men faithfully lay in wait in their boat. They never went to sleep at the same time. Two of them were always awake while the others slept. They were ready to go back to *The Metrova* as soon as Daffodil and her companions arrived.

A light went on in the Captain's cabin immediately Kø heard Daffodil's footsteps, and he was on the deck and waiting before the eight of them finished climbing aboard. He ushered them to his cabin where Boussy, Hololegs and King Mingo also sat waiting. They huddled together and listened intently to Daffodil's account. Kø left the circle and paced slowly up and down his cabin.

"I can't thank you enough, Daffodil and all of you! I can't thank you enough," he paused. "Here's an interesting saying you will appreciate, 'If you think you are too small to make a difference, you haven't spent a night with a mosquito!'"

Everyone laughed!

"Am I the mosquito then?" asked Daffodil laughingly.

"Yes, you are!" replied Kø. "You are a fearless and remarkable one!" said Kø. "And I don't know what we would have done without you!"

"What do we do now?" someone asked.

"There is another saying I love," said Kø thoughtfully. "And it goes like this: "When spider webs unite, they can tie up a lion."

All the people in the room nodded silently.

"It's time to tie up some lions!" he declared.

27

"I wish I could go with you," Katie said to her husband.

She was sitting on a plush, green, velvet *Swedish Biedermeier* birch root sofa. Her two-year-old son, Marc, was lying asleep in her lap. She was in the first trimester of her second pregnancy and though she was generally in good health, the waves of nausea that hit her at the most unexpected times were still most disconcerting.

Her husband, General Sønne, had recently started a large dairy farm on the outskirts of Copenhagen. Denmark was striving to be among the top five milk producing nations in the world, and he wanted to be among the top five dairy farmers in the country. Though he had a very good manager, he insisted on going there every fortnight or so to make sure that everything was working well and going according to plan. He was a soldier through and through, and it was important for him to make sure, that in this new endeavor, he could create a team he could trust. He wanted his team to have the same vision as he did for getting the job done and making the business as profitable as possible.

It was late afternoon, and the General decided to take a leisurely ride out of Copenhagen and into the countryside. He would arrive there a little after dark, relax, have supper, meet with his manager, and go over the books before going to bed.

His mind was totally on business as he kissed his wife and son goodbye. He settled back to enjoy a leisurely six-hour coach drive to Jutland. His thoughts were on branding and marketing his milk, butter and cheeses. He had no idea when he dozed off. He was jolted into wakefulness when the horses neighed and reared suddenly. Without warning, the carriage jerked to a stop. Captain Sønne thought he heard his coachman curse and he lifted the curtain to check on what was happening. Three elegantly dressed women in hoods and balaclavas met his eyes. The balaclavas were thick and black, and they covered their faces and noses. Black eyes stared at him. Before he could shout, a hand went over his mouth, and he inhaled the contents of a soporific sponge, imbued with narcotics. Simultaneously, a hood was placed over his head, and two pairs of strong arms carried him roughly to another coach. Before he landed on the seat inside the second coach, the General had passed out.

28

Hugo was very happy with the way the evening's meeting went. There were many things to be learned at the Philosopher, Soren Kierkegaard's meetings, and he was happy he had attended this particular meeting. Kierkegaard had said something that really resonated with him, and he couldn't stop thinking about it. The great philosopher said:

"Face the facts of being what you are, for that is what changes what you are."

It seemed to make no sense, but at the same time, the more he thought about it, the better sense it made.

"Face the facts of being what you are, for that is what changes what you are."

Hugo turned it over and over in his mind.

"Who am I?" he asked himself.

"What am I?" he pondered.

Hugo had also purchased a book that Kierkegaard had recently published called **Either/Or**. The book was filled with examples of people at the crossroads of their lives just as he was. For many years now, Hugo constantly felt he was at the crossroads of his life. He felt so torn about his future and whether to continue to work with his father or pursue his own passions. He felt like *The Ugly Duckling* in Hans Andersen's fairy tale who felt he didn't belong anywhere. He slowly walked toward his carriage.

Though Hugo heard the wheels of a carriage rumble and clank somewhere behind him, he assumed the carriage would pass him by. His thoughts were still on the Philosopher's words when the carriage slowed down to a halt beside him. He turned swiftly when a female voice called out to him.

"Hugo Quist!"

Hugo stopped in surprise, trying to place the voice. A lady he didn't recognize walked toward him, distracting him. He was caught flatfooted with astonishment when a pistol was thrust into his side.

"Silence!" was all a gruff voice said as the butt of the pistol pushed him into a waiting carriage.

29

"When will you spend all night with me and not have to go home?" Gerda asked pouting.

Herbert was a great lover. He was kind, considerate and generous. But Gerda was tired of living in the shadows of his family and his wife. Poor thing, Gerda thought shamelessly, Herbert's wife had died recently along with their son. In fact, they had just been buried. They had succumbed to the cholera outbreak that had ravaged the country. It wasn't anyone's fault.

Gerda had been Herbert's lover ever since he came back from Africa two years earlier. She felt she had waited around long enough, and she had no intention of waiting around much longer now that the coast was clear.

"Soon, Gerda soon!" said Herbert lighting a cigarette. "Just be patient till things fall into place."

He lazily lay across the rumpled bed, relishing in the passionate abandon of their recent lovemaking. He hated having to leave, but though his wife was dead, his baby daughter was still alive. His mother had told him that she wasn't too well, so he needed to go home and make sure she was all right.

Herbert looked like a tall, bronzed, Greek god when he finally got out of Gerda's bed. Gerda stared admiringly at the hard muscles in his chest, and she salivated over the hard muscles of his buttocks. She wished she could run her hands all over him again and she pouted and sighed when he got dressed. She would have liked to make love with him again! But it was not to be. He was going home. As usual.

"I will see you tomorrow, my love," he called out airily as he kissed her goodbye. He bounded down the stairs with the energy of a boy half his age. He had not even taken a dozen steps from Gerda's front door when a youthful voice called out his name.

"Mr. Quist, Sir," the youth said politely. "Miss Flora wants to see you. She is the coach over there!"

"At this time of night?" asked Herbert alarmed.

He knew Flora very well. He used to call on her before he married, but his parents didn't approve of their union because, as they put it, "She did not come from 'good stock.' Fortunately or unfortunately, she finally married a boring Lutheran Minister.

"She says it's very urgent!" the youth said accompanying Herbert to a coach parked in a park shielded by trees not too far away.

If Flora needed him, Herbert would drop everything to help her. He doubled his steps, opened the door to the coach and poked his head into the dark interior. He could only assume that it was the youth who shoved him from behind. As he fell headlong into the coach, he opened his mouth to protest.

"If I were you, Herbert," a gruff male voice spoke politely, "I would be quiet!"

Herbert attempted to say something. A bandage went over his mouth, and a hood went over his head. Ropes went over his hands and feet and bound them tightly.

"If I were you, Herbert Quist," the voice repeated ominously, "I would be quiet."

Herbert slumped against the seat in the dark and shut up.

30

Harald was an unapologetic workaholic. His job was not only to manage and oversee the largest of his father's four factories, he was also in charge of the export wing of all the factories. As if that wasn't enough, he found himself overseeing more than his fair share. His father, Hans, was getting older and wasn't in the best of health. Herbert, his brother, was a genius at business; but he was much more interested in women and bedroom matters than the matters of the boardroom. As for Hugo, Harald despaired as he thought about his brother. The boy was more interested in philosophy and poetry than business. "Poetry, ugh!" He thought disparagingly.

Harald decided that he had the curse of the firstborn. He felt that it was always up to him as the firstborn son to do everything that wasn't done by his siblings, and he had to do it well. He sighed as he looked at the clock on the wall of his office. It was just a few minutes to midnight. If only he could plow through the pile of work he had in front of him, he would have less to do tomorrow. So he determinedly worked through the pile of paperwork. It was three in the morning the next time Harald lifted his head up. Weariness drooped his eyelids and stretched his muscles taut. He closed his files and dragged himself to his coach. He had let his coachman go home earlier because the man had to come back in the morning. Harald's home was merely a half an hour away, but he wished someone could take the reins, so he could catch some sleep no matter how uncomfortable.

The horse plodded along, and the cool night air swirled around Harald's head making him sleepier. As he got to a dangerous curve along the road, he slowed down considerably. Suddenly, a group of men leaped out of the shadows, surrounded his coach and had him tied, hooded and bundled before Harald had any time to think. He was furious. This was surely a kidnapping. The audacious fools who did this would have to pay! How dare they try to kidnap him? He was sure they would want a handsome ransom. Once the ransom was paid, he would find them and make them pay it back ten times over! As quickly as it began, all movement ceased. Suddenly, someone pinched his nose. He struggled to breathe. When they let go of his nostrils, he took in huge gulps of air and breathed in noxious fumes. Harald was already out cold by the time he took his second breath.

31

General Sønne let out a long, low groan as he came out of his drug-induced slumber a few hours later. He felt like a dozen enthusiastic African drummers were dancing a war dance on his head. He tried to put his hands on his temple to calm the cacophony. It was then that he realized that his hands and feet were bound to the chair he was sitting in.

"Hvad helvede!" he swore. "What the hell!"

Herbert thought he recognized the voice. He cocked his head.

"Hvad helvede!" the General swore again.

"General Sønne?" Herbert exclaimed. "Is that you, General Sønne?"

"Who is this?" asked the General imperiously.

"Herbert…. it's Herbert Quist," he answered

Harald and Hugo jerked their heads forward and said in unison

"You're here Herbert?" asked Hugo.

"Is that Harald?" asked Herbert.

"What are you doing here?"

"Can someone tell me what the hell is going on?" shouted General Sønne, straining against the ropes.

Someone suddenly yanked the hoods off the heads of the four men. They blinked rapidly as their eyes became accustomed to the dim light. There were five chairs in the small room, arranged in a circle, but only four were occupied. The fifth man who had taken off their hoods was a dark stern looking man who stood behind them like an executioner. The four men looked at each other in dismay. It seemed they were in a small cabin on a ship. There were portholes they couldn't see out of, and they looked at one another in abject wonder.

"How did you get here?" asked Harald.

Just then, the door of the cabin opened. The four seated men looked incredulously at the man that entered the cabin.

"Kø?" they shouted in unison.

"*Det er sgu rigtigt!*" I'll be damned!

"*For helvede!* Goddammit!"

"Lort! Shit!"

"Yes, it's I," said Kø pleasantly as he took a seat. "The man you threw overboard, General Sønne!"

"Here I am!" he said to his brothers. "The very brother you wanted dead!"

There were eight men standing just outside the door waiting to do Kø's bidding. Boussy stood behind Kø. His face was expressionless, but his piercing black eyes gave away the intense dislike he felt for the four men. His muscles were bulging, and he flexed them slowly and ominously for their benefit.

Kø studied each of his brothers. They tried, but couldn't meet his eyes. Then his eyes rested on the General:

"I can understand a man's jealousy when he thinks another has touched his woman, General Sønne," he said. "But surely, as a soldier, shouldn't you have given me a chance to explain before you condemned me to death?"

The General opened and closed his mouth rapidly like a dying fish. He was still in shock at the sight of Kø. He was sure that Kø had drowned in the ocean. How did he survive? How did he get to Denmark? How did he find them? Trouble has come to Copenhagen, he thought.

"Well, General," Kø said in a low matter of fact voice, 'he who pelts another with pebbles asks for stones in return'!"

"I'm so sorry!" the General finally said lamely. "I was jealous. I am sorry!"

Kø looked at his brothers.

"I can understand a man's jealousy when he thinks another has touched his woman," he repeated, "but what I cannot understand is, how brothers can stand back and watch someone

286

attempt to kill their brother and decide to do nothing about it! You were there…you saw everything… and yet you decided to do nothing at all."

"We're sorry…." began Hugo.

"Why?" Kø asked as though he had not heard Hugo speak.

There was no answer

"Is it because of who I am?"

No answer.

"Is it because of who my mother is?"

There was some uncomfortable squirming in the chairs.

"Isn't it enough that we have one father?"

There was a palpable pause.

"And isn't it enough that the same blood that flows through our father's veins, flows through your veins and mine as well?"

Three men looked at their bound feet.

"Am I not your brother? Am I not a man like you? Did not one God create us all?"

The men looked at one another and looked at their feet again.

Tears came from nowhere and ran down Kø's face.

"My blood isn't black, you know… it's red…. like yours….like Papi's."

There was a long pause before he continued: "….and it's red, just like my mother's!"

"Kø," whispered Hugo. "I'm sorry!"

"I'm sorry," stuttered General Sønne, "very sorry, very sorry… Katie explained it all to me in the end."

The other brothers muttered apologies.

Kø angrily clenched and unclenched his fists. His eyes took on a faraway look. When he spoke again, his voice took on that commanding tone which Boussy remembered.

"Boussy," Kø said, "throw them overboard! Let them have a taste of what it feels like to face death."

As he exited the room, he ignored their protests and said to the eight men waiting outside…

"We shall do it one man at a time…starting with the General!"

Two of King Mingo's men came into the room and untied the General, hands and feet. The general protested loudly as he was led to the deck.

"Listen, Kø," said Harald, "we are sorry. I am sorry."

"Yes," said Hugo, "I am truly sorry! We are really sorry we did nothing to help you."

As the door closed shut, General Sønne earnestly pleaded for his life.

"Katie is pregnant, Kø! We have a little son…I'll give you anything you want, Kø… anything! Just tell me what you want!"

"Well, let's talk about this then," Kø said pleasantly taking a seat.

"Now tell me, is this just you, negotiating for your life, or are my dear brothers also interested in this deal?"

His brothers drew closer to the General, and the five men huddled close together. Four spoke earnestly, and one stroked his chin from time to time looking each of them in the eye, asking questions and negotiating until he was satisfied with the deal.

"Fetch King Mingo will you, Boussy?" Boussy was the only one who was in the room with Kø, and he trotted off to find the man.

"So will you let us go now?" the General asked.

"Not on your life!" Kø exclaimed. "Not until you give me everything as promised!"

"How do we know you won't kill us once you get everything we spoke about?"

"Well, you'll never really know what I'm capable of, will you? I guess you'll just have to trust me."

"King Mingo," he said as King Mingo appeared. At three hundred and fifty pounds and six foot four, King Mingo exuded a commanding aura. He was the dark kind of African, whose skin tone could best be described as midnight, and his intense dislike for the four men was apparent in his deep scowl. They looked at him in awe, and he scowled even deeper, until the furrows between his brows looked like jagged ancient tribal marks.

"Lock these people up in separate cabins until I come back," Kø told him.

Then he turned to Boussy and said, "Let's get ready, we have to take a trip into Copenhagen"

32

Mingo was tasked with overseeing the affairs of *The Metrova,* assisted by Ezekiel while Kø, Boussy and Daffodil went ashore. Daffodil looked like a princess in her pale yellow day gown. She wore a gold earring and necklace set that Mark had given her after one of their trysts. The contents of her yellow purse were known to no-one but Daffodil herself.

For the first time in almost two decades, Kø decided to have his hair cut. It was fashionably cut to a length just below the collar of his shirt. It was parted on the side, slicked back and combed to a high wave at the center of his forehead.

Ezekiel the tailor, made expert alterations to Boussy's clothing to accommodate his thick neck and the rippling muscles of his arms and thighs. The men's shirts, made of the finest linen, had high upstanding collars. The plaid fabric of their straight legged full-length trousers matched their waistcoats. Daffodil reminded them to make sure the bottom button of the waistcoat was undone for ease when sitting. The four-in-hand neckties were tied in a perfect knot with the pointed ends sticking out. Both men topped it off with the sack coat, which was a loosely fitting, mid-thigh length coat.

"Stop fiddling with your necktie," Kø said to Boussy as he handed him a top hat. Boussy sheepishly took his finger away from between his neck and his starched collar. Instead, he ground his teeth at the discomfort the restriction was causing his neck. To distract himself, he admired his black, highly polished leather boots, the first he had ever owned.

Kø fixed a pocket watch to his waistcoat and looked at the time. Together, the trio left early that morning to finish the task that had taken Kø almost three years to accomplish - the visit to his father.

Magnus was faithfully waiting when they got to the shore, and Daffodil gave him a hug and a kiss on his cheek. Magnus, flustered, flushed to the roots of his hair. Kø, Daffodil, and Boussy settled back in the horsedrawn carriage and admired the plush interior. Kø fingered his pocket watch, Daffodil removed her shawl and looked out of the window and Boussy resisted the urge to put his finger under his tight collar. Instead, he clenched his teeth till the moment of discomfort passed.

Kø and Boussy's eyes were as wide as new moons when they saw the three, four and even five-storey buildings that lined the streets. The coachman weaved through the cobbled streets of Copenhagen as he showed them the sights. To Magnus' chagrin, all three passengers, burst out laughing when he showed them the new brewery. They remembered the Pirate Peegee and the coup Daffodil had accomplished in ensuring that the pirates would be sick to their stomachs, and unable to leave their fort, while they made their getaway from the island. There were peals of laughter when Daffodil told Magnus the story. It was only when they got to Valby Train Station, that they all stopped the chatter. The moment of reckoning was almost at hand! It wouldn't be long now. Kø was about to meet his father face to face!

When they finally got to the address, the house was so imposing that for a few moments, Kø wasn't sure whether to go in or not. After a few minutes of indecision, he decided that this wasn't something that needed to be negotiated or deliberated upon. He swallowed his trepidation and determinedly ran up the few stairs that led to the front of the house. He held the brass knocker and hesitated. Like sentinels, Daffodil and Boussy stood beside him, one on each side. With a deep breath, Kø dropped the knocker. It gave a loud thump, and the door opened almost immediately. A stooped, elderly doorman peered out at them from the tops of his half-moon glasses.

The marble floor was highly polished, and from where Kø stood, he could see a hallway illuminated by lamps on metal pillars with petal-shaped shades. Two staircases curved majestically upward, like arms, imperiously beckoning one to the second floor of the mansion. Looking past the doorman, Kø could just make out a stucco of paintings, sculpture, ironwork and decorations. Kø cricked his neck and saw, that hanging from a ceiling which seemed to be at least two storeys high, was the largest, most intricate candelabra he had ever seen! His Pa lived in a palace, he suddenly realized. He cleared his throat nervously.

"I would like to see Mr. Hans Quist," he stated.

"He isn't in at this time," the doorman said.

From inside the house, a baby started wailing.

"We would like to wait for him," Kø continued.

The baby wailed louder. A soft voice tried to calm it down. Hurried footsteps went to and fro, not far from where they stood.

"Is he expecting you?" the doorman asked, ignoring the baby's cries.

"No, he isn't. But it's most important that we see him."

"That is not possible!" stated the doorman firmly. "Without an appointment, it is just not possible to see Mr. Quist!"

"It has to be possible!' Kø cried. "I cannot leave without seeing him! Please tell him he has visitors from Africa!" Kø stated.

At the commotion, footsteps approached the front door.

"Who is it, Anton?" a soft, well-modulated voice asked.

"Some people from Africa who want to see the master," said the doorman, "but they don't have an appointment."

A tall, slender lady, dressed in mourning, approached them. She wore black from neck to toe. Her hair was put up in a simple bun, but the shock of white hair at her temple broke the melancholy of her mourning clothes. Her eyes were red-rimmed with crying, but she held her head high as she glided to the doorway.

"How can we help you?" she asked.

"We are here to see Mr. Hans Quist," Kø repeated.

"He had an early morning appointment, so he isn't here. But what's your ...?" the lady began.

A shrill cry interrupted her question, and a harried-looking nanny came to the door holding a screaming child. The nanny held a large napkin to the baby's mouth as the baby alternatively screamed and retched pitifully. The baby's skin looked dry and parched and her blue/grey eyes, when she was able to open them, were dull and sunken.

The woman's attention was divided between Kø and the baby.

"What's your name?" she asked again cooing at the baby and wiping her brow and lips with a wet rag she had in her hand.

"My name is Kondo Quist," said Kø. His voice had a stubborn quality to it.

"Madam," interrupted Daffodil, "it seems the baby has cholera, if you don't see to her, you will have a problem on your hands.....a big problem!" she emphasized not wanting to mention the worst.

"Yes, I know, but we have done everything. The disease is everywhere!"

"I can help you," said Daffodil. Her eyes, which were fixed on the child, were full of concern.

"How would you do that? Are you a nurse...?"

"No, I am not but...." began Daffodil.

"What did you say your name was again?" she asked Kø, turning her attention fully to Kø. His name finally registered something in her brain.

"My name is Hans Kondo Quist," said Kø again, emphasizing each word. "And I am here to see my father, Hans Pieter Quist."

Jacoba gasped as she took a good look at Kø. She saw the striking resemblance between the tall young man and her husband. He looked like her husband much more than any of her children did. Hans... she thought...Hans Quist!!! And he was here from Africa! In her mind, she groped for something to hold on to. But the world spun too quickly, and before she knew what was going on, she clutched frantically at air, just before her world turned black.

The doorman stepped back, gasping in horror. He wasn't sure what shocked him most – the news of his master's illegitimate son or his mistress's dead faint. Both Kø and Boussy pushed their way in and caught Jacoba just before she hit the ground. And suddenly, everyone started talking at the same time. The baby's wailing reached an ear-piercing crescendo and Daffodil snatched her from the hands of the nanny and urgently demanded a bowl of hot water, wet sugar and salt as she fished in her purse for medicinal powders. Kø shouted orders to Anton, and limping in an exaggerated way, Anton reluctantly led the way to Jacoba's rooms. The nurse wrung her hands helplessly, running between the baby, her mistress, the kitchen and the visitors. Thus, the trio of strangers brought the Quist house into total disarray that morning.

Daffodil fed the rehydrating mixture to the baby and rocked her gently till she fell asleep. Jacoba was calmed down with a couple of shots of brandy and was encouraged to take some rest. Daffodil thought the nurse needed a shot of brandy too...but she thought it would be probably better if she stayed sober. She just might be needed!

Anton ushered the visitors into the drawing room. The room was scrumptiously decorated. It was designed to impress and awe at first sight! And it did! If Kø had not seen an imposing daguerreotype of his father, stepmother and brothers on the wall, he would have been sure that he was in the wrong place! Nothing in his imagination prepared him for this. Surely, Kø thought, my father is King, and this, is his palace!

With over a dozen ornate chairs in the room, Kø, Boussy, and Daffodil were at a loss as to where to sit. What were a simple man from Africa, a former prince turned slave and a former prostitute doing in a Danish palace? The room looked like an ornament. It was decorated with white and pastel colors combined with gilding in the characteristics of the French *Rococo* style. The family portrait and the many mirrors and paintings that lined the walls were put in complex frames made of plaster of paris and gilded with a brilliant gold.

On the mantel sat a crowd of *chinoiserie,* Chinese vases and ornaments. Several similarly designed tables held all kinds of ornaments that had been collected from all over the world. There were a pair of sphinx from Egypt, obelisks from Greece and realistic looking marble busts of unknown people.

Kø stared at his surroundings and asked Anton:

"Doesn't Pa have a study here? He always liked to have a study!"

"Most certainly he does." Limping, Anton led the way.

The study was filled with Hans' presence as well as his possessions. At least in here, Kø could breathe freely, and for once, he was able to relax. The walls were all paneled with dark, exotic wood. Most of the furniture in the study was made in the *Papa Biedermeier style,* which originated in Germany and Austria. The chairs were made with mahogany or cherry wood and had curved legs. The upholstery of the sofa was soft, deep and generous.

Kø took a seat on a sofa, and Boussy and Daffodil sat on either side of him. Together, they gazed at the imposing portraits of Hans, Jacoba, his sons, daughters-in-law and seven grandchildren that occupied most of one wall. Books lined another wall from floor to ceiling, and though his father's library in Quitta had several books, it was nothing like this. Kø was impressed by the sheer number of books his father possessed. The writing table in the corner was inlaid with gold. A couple of exquisite old quills and modern fountain pens and an inkwell sat on the table. The shelves on the opposite wall held models of different kinds of ships. They stared at the different ships, and marveled at how exquisite the miniatures were. They almost missed one of the ships, which was almost hidden. It was hiding behind two warships built in different centuries.

"I made that ship!" said Kø jumping to his feet in surprise and delight.

"I made it for my father when I was about twelve years old!" he laughed and carefully picked it up.

"How ugly it looks!" he exclaimed.

It was his first attempt at carpentry, and the miniature was badly made. He remembered how he forced the wood to obey him, rather than let its grain speak to him and guide his design. Kø smiled at the recollection as he picked up the ship and looked underneath it. There, underneath the model, was the inscription he had made with his own hands:

Daffodil read the roughly inscribed words.

"For Pa-pigen. From your son, Hans."

Kø put the ship back in its place as memories flooded his head and overwhelmed him. He finally took a seat at a vantage point where he could see anyone who entered the house. He felt he had to be prepared to meet the unknown. His outward calm belied the way he tapped his thumbs together. Tap, tap tap tap….. Only someone who knew him well would know that Kø's emotions were broiling. Taptap, taptaptap. Boussy squeezed his shoulder. Daffodil squeezed his hand and said nothing. It seemed there were just not enough words to language their feelings.

It wasn't very long before several carriages approached the door. From their vantage point, Kø, Daffodil, and Boussy could see the carriages stop just in front of the main doors. As the carriage doors opened, Kø stood up. His hands hung loosely by his sides as though he had forgotten they existed. His friends stood as close to him as possible. The butler opened the door. An entourage of about six people all dressed in somber black slowly entered the drawing room.

From the open doorway of the study, Kø saw the tall, handsome figure of his father. For a moment, his heart stopped. Kø realized he hadn't seen his father in almost a decade! When he removed his top hat, Kø saw with shock that his father's hair had changed from blond to silver. There wasn't a speck of blond hair in sight. Kø thought he walked with a slight limp, but he covered it up quite well when he leaned on his walking cane. Kø stood rooted to the spot, desperately willing his heart to stop its' over anxious antics. Just then, the butler bent close to Hans and whispered into his ear. He gestured briefly toward the study. Hans's head snapped back at the information he had been given and shock and disbelief registered on his face.

"My son! Kø-Pigen!" he cried weeping, taking long strides toward his son with outstretched arms.

"Is that you? Is this really you? I thought you were dead! They told me you went overboard in a storm!"

Father and son took long strides, met in the middle of the room, and enveloped each other in a tight embrace. They squeezed their eyes shut, but that didn't prevent their emotions from spilling and overflowing. Captain Laarsen, one of the guests, stood rooted to the spot, staring in disbelief at the apparition standing in front of him.

There was more commotion at the door, as a woman's voice called Kø's name. She sounded as though she was asking a question.

"Kø!" she screamed again. This time, the name sounded like a prolonged wail somewhere between pain, wonder and incredulity. There, among the small crowd, was Katie. She looked even lovelier if possible as she held the hand of a little curly-haired, blue-eyed boy. Her hands flew to her mouth and then she covered her eyes unable to believe that the man she had seen being thrown overboard was standing right there in front of her. "He must be a ghost!" she thought frantically. "He

MUST be a ghost!" She took another incredible look at Kø and promptly fell into a dead swoon!

A gentleman of mixed parentage caught her just before she hit the ground. Katie's son started to wail at the sight of his mother on the floor. The poor boy thought his mother was going to be put in a box and buried, just like the mother of the other child and his fear was palpable. Daffodil rushed to the boy's side, picked him up and comforted the weeping child, while the man of mixed parentage bent to assist Katie. He carried her as though she was a child.

"Where do I put her?" he addressed Daffodil directly for some reason.

She looked at him, about to retort, when something clutched hard at her heart. For Daffodil, who had never been shy of any man since she was thirteen, she felt a shyness she couldn't understand. The man couldn't take his eyes off her and his eyes burned into her soul. For a moment, he forgot he was carrying Katie and Daffodil forgot she was carrying Katie's son. It was as though they were alone in the room. Their eyes asked questions of each other, but before the questions were answered, their hearts began to meld together.

All the while, Captain Laarsen stood at the door, with his heart in his mouth. With Kø looking larger than life, standing in his father's house, he knew he was in trouble. Big trouble, because he was the one who had told Hans that Kø had gone overboard in the storm.

"Mikkel?" Hans questioned Captain Laarsen. He made an imperious questioning gesture with his hand.

Captain Laarsen bowed his head, looked for words of explanation and found none.

"I demand an explanation, Mikkel!"

Mikkel Laarsen shook his head slowly, unable to speak. How could he language his true feelings about the situation? How could he? How could he tell Hans that it was wrong to bring an illegitimate child to Copenhagen and into his marital home? A black child at that!!! Indeed, in a strange sense, Kø wasn't illegitimate because Hans had married Kø's mother in the little Lutheran church in Quitta. Mikkel Laarsen was a witness when the Danish minister married them. It was all very complicated. How could Hans announce his crime of bigamy to polite society? Who in Denmark could understand the life one led and the decisions one made in Africa? How could Hans successfully bring his seemingly duplicitous past into his impeccable present? How would his history affect his and everyone's future? Kø was living testimony to Hans' life on the Guinea Coast and Mikkel Laarsen believed that Hans should understand exactly how he felt. He began to feel anger at his friend for putting him on the spot. Try as he might, Captain Laarsen couldn't find the accurate words to language his thoughts. Haltingly, he tried to give voice to his fears and concerns... words failed him. He looked imploringly at his friend of over forty years. Finally, Hans helped him out.

"I know what you can't say Mikkel," said Hans. "You don't know this, but I confessed everything to Jacoba. I had to confess after my stroke, so there would be no surprises if I were to die. It was very difficult, but we made peace about it. But whatever the circumstances are, Kø is my son, Mikkel, my flesh... my blood. I couldn't deny him or any of my children for any reason!"

The one thing Mikkel Laarsen didn't know and couldn't fathom was the depth of love that Hans had for his son. This son.

It was a love that defied all conventions, all norms and mores, and all man-made taboos.

33

It took a long time for the people in the Quist household to simmer down after Katie fainted. She came around after a few minutes and started crying all over again when she saw Kø. It was only then, that the truth about what really happened aboard *The Pharaoh* was revealed to Hans. Kø filled his father in on the rest of his adventures and how Boussy and Daffodil had saved his life.

"You can't leave this afternoon," said Kø's father said to him in a determined, matter of fact way.

"But I have a ship full of people waiting for me," Kø said stubbornly.

"There is no way I can let you leave! Not just yet," his father emphasized. I asked you to come because there are some things we needed to discuss!"

"You didn't ask me to come, Pa, I decided to see you myself!" Kø retorted

"Didn't you see the telegraph?" his father asked patiently.

"What telegraph?"

"The telegraph I sent to Captain Laarsen asking him to bring you to Copenhagen."

"You sent a telegraph to Captain Laarsen asking me to come see you?" Kø asked incredulously.

"Mikkel!!!!" Kø's father bellowed calling out for Captain Laarsen. He had a brandy glass at his elbow, and he took a couple of swigs. The doctor had advised against drinking and smoking after his stroke a few years earlier. He had given both up, but today was an unusual day, and he just needed a little extra fortification.

"The Captain just left," said Conrad Wulff, the man of mixed parentage, as he poked his head into the study.

Hans settled back in his chair. He had started the day by sorting out the affairs of his recently deceased daughter-in-law and grandchild. Then, the son he thought he had lost forever, showed up. What a day! It started with grief and ended with astonishment and joy. He looked at his son and smiled.

"Yes, Kø, I did," he answered, "I sent a telegraph asking Captain Laarsen to bring you to Copenhagen to see me."

Kø looked out of the window and into the formal gardens beyond the curtains in the study. He still couldn't believe he was finally in his father's house. He had no idea that his father had actually sent for him. He had thought that Captain Laarsen had allowed him on the ship just because he asked. How naïve he was! But his heart was glad to hear that his father did send for him.

"Kø-pigen," Hans said gently, "please stay for just one week.... just seven days. There are many things we need to discuss. There are things I want to show you. I haven't seen you in almost a decade!"

From where Kø sat, he could see Daffodil in the garden listening to an earnest Conrad Wulff. Their heads were close together, and Kø wondered vaguely what they were talking about. His thoughts wandered to General Sønne and his brothers. Before long, their absence would be felt, and Kø was certain they would make him pay for kidnapping them. Meanwhile, his father was waiting for an answer.

"Of course, Pa, I'll stay," said Kø, "if you could arrange for Boussy to take some supplies to *The Metrova* and let King Mingo and the others know the new arrangements, I will definitely stay!"

34

The following day, Jacoba was still feeling unwell, so Hans had carried a breakfast tray up to her himself. He saw to it that she ate something before he came down to have breakfast with Kø.

Hans was quiet when he sat with her. He knew she would voice her concerns and her feelings and he gave her the time and space to articulate them.

"He looks very much like you," she said quietly.

"Yes. I know." He stretched out his hand and touched hers gently.

"Same height, same body, same smile...."

"Yes..."

"Almost like an exact copy of you...'

He moved and sat next to her and gripped her hand tightly.

"I know you told me all about it," she said slowly, "but seeing him in person was unexpected... surprising... and...painful."

309

"I know," he said continuing to hold her hand tightly. There was a long silence before he spoke.

"I'm sorry," he said simply.

"It was like seeing a shadow of you…very disconcerting."

"I can only imagine. I'm sorry I hurt you." He said

She was quiet. He didn't relax his grip on her hand.

"Life can only be understood backwards," He said finally, "but it must be lived forwards…I can't make any excuses, Jacoba. I stand accused, and I accept my guilt. What I humbly ask, is that you forgive me and trust me. He *is* my son, and I love him as I love all our sons. Trust me as you did the first time we met."

He held her as she quietly wept.

"I want you to know, that I would never intentionally hurt you."

"Can you trust me, *min elskede*[28]? He asked. It was a long time before she spoke.

"I choose to trust you," she said.

Daffodil, Kø and his father were just finishing breakfast when Katie came in with little Marc in tow.

"I would like to invite Daffodil to stay with me for a few days if you don't mind, Kø," Katie said as she joined them at the breakfast table.

---

[28] Danish for 'My beloved'

"I'm sure you and your father have a lot to talk about. My husband is away at his farm, and I would like to get to know Daffodil, take her shopping and maybe take her to see more of the city if I may."

Daffodil and Kø exchanged a surreptitious look but said nothing. So it was all arranged. Conrad Wulff drove Daffodil to Katie's home later that morning, while Kø sat in the study to talk with his father.

They were quiet for a while as they settled in.

"I wanted to know...."

"Tell me...."

Both men began to speak at the same time. They stopped, looked at each other and laughed.

"There is so much to say, isn't there, Kø- Pigen, and you have so many questions. I know that."

Kø nodded.

"Go ahead, ask."

"Why did you leave Quitta without saying goodbye to me, Pa?" Kø asked. Finally, he asked the question that had been on his mind for almost a decade.

Hans carefully selected a *Figurado* cigar from his humidor. He went through the motions of cutting and moistening the tip of the cigar, smelling it, and lighting it. And then he sat back and puffed in and out, as he enjoyed the deep, musky fragrance.

"You should try one," Hans said.

Kø laughed. "I will…. show me how."

Father showed son what to do, and both men settled deep into the plush sofas smoking and enjoying a silent companionship.

"I was the first of seven children, you know," Hans began.

"I didn't know that!" Kø interjected. "I thought you were an only child!"

"In a way, I was…. but no, I wasn't an only child."

"But how can that be, Pa?"

"When I was three or four, my mother had a baby. Carl was his name. He was my baby brother, and I adored him. Just when he was old enough to run and play with me, he died. I don't remember now what it was that killed him. But that pattern continued. By the time I was fourteen, my mother had had five more children. None of them lived past the age of two or three. They all died as a result of some childhood ailment. Unfortunately, my parents were too poor to get them the medical help they needed.

For years, poverty and death were the only things that were constant around me….and those tragedies changed the way I perceived life. I saw my mother's despair grow and my father's disappointment escalate. I understood how devastating poverty could be. My father needed sons to help him when he went fishing. He needed sons to help him on his farm. I hated anything to do with fishing or farming or any manual labor for that matter. For a long time, I think, to my father, I, the one who lived, was the biggest disappointment of all!

"There were a few things that losing my siblings taught me...the first was that, life... any life, is precious. This is why I don't believe in discrimination of any kind. A human being is a human being. A gift to the universe for reasons we might not understand. And it's not our place to stand in judgment of any human being for any reason.

"Poverty taught me that education is the most important gift one can give to oneself and one's children. Not only formal education, you know; life itself gives many lessons. If we know how to listen, the universe has lessons of its own. We can also learn from others who have spent time in introspection and experimentation. And if we make the quest for knowledge a lifelong one, knowledge will be like a guiding hand to offer us the best that life has to give."

"I will always remember that, Pa," said Kø. He was glad he had stayed.

"And finally I also learned that no-one knows how long one is given, so whatever one does, one should never procrastinate!"

Hans paused as he tapped his cigar gently against the side of the ashtray.

"I was very determined never to be poor, no matter what it took!" He paused again, laid his head against the head of the chair, cigar temporarily forgotten.

"It drove me to think the unimaginable, do the inconceivable and attain the implausible."

Hans paused and took several puffs of his cigar. He contemplated the cigars glowing tip for so long that Kø thought he had finished his explanation.

"But that still doesn't explain why you left..." Kø insisted.

"Patience, my son, patience."

Hans pointed to a decanter.

"Pour me a drink, will you, Kø, and pour one for yourself."

Kø poured a small finger of brandy into his father's snifter and the same for himself.

Hans took several sips and picked up the conversation from where he left off.

"You know, parents are just adults who happen to have children. We have our ambitions and aspirations and our faults and limitations. We want to do the right thing for ourselves and for our children at the same time. The only thing is that those two desires don't always fit together at the same time."

Kø tried to digest his father's words.

"All my life, I wanted two things - money and power."

"But you had both, Pa!"

"I thought so for a while, until I received word from the King inviting me to be a part of the Council of State. It was the highest honor the King could give. You see, it was one of the most ludicrous dreams I had when I was a young man. And suddenly, that dream was coming true! For someone like me, it was the ultimate honor, and nothing mattered more than that."

Hans continued. "Do you remember you the trip with you went on with your mother and uncle?"

"I remember the day very well!"

"In a way, I was glad you had gone on the trip, because you were always so melancholic each time I traveled. At the time, I reasoned that it was the best thing for all of us. So I dropped everything and left. I intended to write to you and your mother, once I settled down, but then I had a stroke which affected my right arm and couldn't write."

There was a knock on the door, and both men jumped in surprise.

"Anton?" Hans called out.

The old butler came in shuffling his feet.

"You have a visitor sir," he intoned. "Mrs. Helene, Mr. Harald's wife is here. She insists she must see you immediately. She is in the drawing room, sir."

Hans gave a small frown. He didn't want to be disturbed. But Helene wasn't a fussy type of woman, so if she insisted on seeing him, she must have a good reason.

There was another knock just as Anton finished delivering the message and he limped to the front door as quickly as he could. Gerda pushed past Anton as soon as the door opened. She waltzed in, swaying her hips provocatively. Her lips were painted a deep red color that matched the deep red dress she was wearing. There was a force about her that didn't take no for an answer and Anton didn't have the strength to push back on her imperious query. He led her to the drawing room to meet Hans even though he realized that he had broken protocol.

"To what do I owe this unexpected but extraordinary pleasure?" asked Hans looking from one woman to the other. The atmosphere in the room was hostile. There was no love lost between Helene and Gerda. And even though Herbert's wife had sadly passed away, his sordid affair with Gerda was an open secret that had caused his deceased wife a lot of heartache. But the matter at hand needed urgent attention and Helene didn't waste time on any niceties.

"Harald didn't come home last night Mr. Quist," Helene began. "He usually works late, so I thought nothing about it. I called at the office, and they hadn't seen him. I just wondered whether you would know his whereabouts."

"Well, well," said Gerda in her brash way. "I came here for the same reason! Herbert was expected at a meeting but didn't make it. I came to find out if you would know where he might be, Mr. Quist!"

"These are grown men! Surely, they cannot be missing," retorted Hans.

"I will find out what is going on... but don't worry, I am sure it's just a small mix up."

Anton let Gerda out, but Helene decided to visit with Jacoba for a while. When Hans went back into the study, Kø was helping himself to another cigar.

"What is it, Pa?"

"Nothing to worry about Kø, I'll get to it later. Where were we?" Hans asked picking up his cigar. It had burned out while he was away, and he sat back, lit it and took his time to enjoy its dark rich aroma.

"You were telling me about the King and the telegraph," Kø reminded him.

35

It was in the summer of 1846 that Hans arrived at the palace in Copenhagen. This was a dream come true and he walked on air. The King had absolute power. He had the supreme authority over everything, and his word was law. This was the opportunity of a life time. Finally, Hans walked in the corridors of power. He had the ear of the King and ruled with him.

For over a year, Hans was constantly in the palace. His businesses were thriving under the able administration of his sons. His home was a peaceful haven. Jacoba made sure of that. Denmark was thriving under the able administration of the King and his close circle of advisors. There was nothing more that Hans wanted in life....till the king died at the end of 1847 and everything changed.

Hans could never explain what happened to him that day in 1847, the day the King died. He had breakfast as usual with Jacoba, and they lingered at the table sharing a little time together before he left to attend to matters of state. He had been suffering from indigestion for a while, and he thought that it was because of all the late night eating and drinking they had been indulging in at the palace. But today, he felt light-headed. The pain in his arm seemed to be creeping up toward his heart.

"Jacoba!" Hans called out.

She continued chatting.

"Jacoba!!" he called out again.

Jacoba had been asking his opinion about something. She waited for an answer, on hearing nothing, she looked at him expectantly and saw his mouth was wide open. It was obvious he was trying to speak, but no sound came out. She rushed to his side and reached him just before he slid out of his chair. He was too heavy for her. She screamed his name just as they slid to the floor together.

Hans had a stroke on the day the King died. His recovery and rehabilitation was painful and slow and went well into January 1848, when a new King succeeded the throne.

By June 1848, absolute monarchy was abolished, and a constitutional monarchy was established. The constitution, known as the June Constitution, was altered to create the framework of a constitutional monarchy for Denmark. The new constitution restricted the King's power and Hans was dispensed of all his royal services. He suddenly came face to face with the fact that he was mortal and dispensable. He came to understand that the loose ends of his life needed to be tied and he needed to make peace with his family and his maker. He needed to spend time with each of his sons, get to know them, have them know him, and generally, Hans decided to put his affairs in order. Hans told his wife, Jacoba, about Kø when he was able to speak and asked for her forgiveness. Kø was "an unfinished business," and he needed to find a way to speak to him. That was when Hans sent for Anton, and sent a telegraph to Africa.

"Forgive me Kø-pigen, for not being in touch."

"There is nothing to forgive Pa- pigen."

Before his father left Quitta, Kø knew him as a boy could know a father. Now, he understood his father as a man. The trip and all he had suffered was certainly worth it.

36

For five glorious days, Father and son were inseparable. It was like the old days in Quitta, when Kø was a boy. Then, they went everywhere together. Hans took Kø to see the sights in Copenhagen. He took him to meet his grandmother, Bedstemor. Unfortunately, his grandfather had passed away in late 1851. His grandmother cooked a meal for him, and constantly ruffled his hair, amazed at how curly it was.

On the way back home, Kø wanted to make sure that Daffodil was all right, so they went to the General and Katie's house. There, sitting on a love seat, holding hands, were Daffodil and Conrad. Kø stared at the two of them in astonishment. They couldn't take their eyes or hands off each other! He had never seen Daffodil so taken with anyone before.

"What's going on here, Daffodil?" Kø asked in bewilderment.

"I don't think I..." began Daffodil.

"Kø, Hans, could you please sit down for a minute?" asked Conrad Wulff.

Once everyone made themselves comfortable, Kø couldn't be more astonished at the words that came out of Conrad's mouth, "I would like to ask your permission, as her big brother, Kø, to ask Daffodil to marry me," he said putting his arm around her.

Kø's jaw dropped in consternation.

"That's a question only Daffodil can answer," he said looking at Daffodil.

"I would very much like to marry Conrad." She said, "but there are many things we need to discuss.

She turned to Conrad, "Kø and I need to talk alone."

As they got home later that evening, three carriages were lined outside Hans' house. In the morning room were four women: Jacoba, Gerda, and Harald's wife Helene and Hugo's wife. After perfunctory greetings Kø excused himself. He made his way to his father's study and helped himself to some brandy. The news of Daffodil's marriage hit him like a ton of bricks. He hadn't properly digested it and he wanted to get away from the crowd and digest this news.

"Daffodil...married?" he shook his head at the thought, "What an unexpected surprise!" he said as he swallowed a large gulp of brandy. He let out a loud gasp as the liquid burned his throat.

He settled down to soberly reflect on this new development, and what it meant for him and for those waiting on *The Metrova*. He had come to rely on Daffodil so much that leaving her behind almost felt like cutting off his right arm. On the other hand, if anyone deserved happiness, it was Daffodil. And Daffodil was the smartest, kindest, most independent person he knew. She was street smart and wise beyond her years. She would be alright. Besides he knew that he could count on his father to watch out for her. With that, Kø relaxed and waited for his father.

It wasn't long before Hans came hurrying in.

"We have to go to the Police station to make a police report, Kø. Your brothers are missing!"

"What? Errrrm, Pa....." Kø said reluctantly.

"Listen, you don't have to come with me, but I have to give a missing person's report..."

"Errrm Pa..."

"I will be back as soon as I can!"

"Papi!!! Could you sit down for a minute please?"

Something in Kø's tone finally got to Hans, but he remained standing.

"Please, don't go to the police, Pa," Kø said slowly. "I know where they are."

"Jeg vil blive fordømt!" "I'll be damned!" Hans exclaimed.

"I have them, Pa," said Kø. "I had to kidnap them, Pa, because I wasn't sure how they would react to me if they found out I was in Copenhagen. I had to get them out of the way, so I could spend time with you. Harald, Hugo and Herbert, and General Laarsen are on my ship."

Just at that moment, Jacoba entered the study. "You...*you* kidnapped my sons?" She said incredulously.

Hans sat heavily, as though he'd been shot!

37

Nothing Hans said could calm Jacoba down. Normally a sweet woman, Hans had never seen her so irate. She swept out of the house with her daughters-in law in tow.

"Take us to the Police station this instance!" she said to the coachman. "I have to report this matter immediately or my name isn't Jacoba Boresen!"

When Hans turned to Kø, his eyes were sad.

"You will have to leave right away Kø-pigen."

"I understand Pa."

Hans opened his safe and took out an old and rusty key. It looked vaguely familiar to Kø, and he turned it over when his father placed it in his hand.

When Hans built the fort in Quitta, he put in a few secret rooms where he could safely keep gold dust and other gems he intended to buy. On the day Kø was born, he decided to leave something for his son because invariably, he knew he would have to leave Africa one day. So he took a small portion of every transaction of precious metals and ornaments he purchased and kept them for him. Kø was speechless when his father explained this to him. There were no words that either man could utter to explain the depth of emotion that they both felt that day. The long embrace they shared spelled everything out. The unshed tears in their eyes as they looked each other over, forever etched the moment in their minds, and gave meaning that words never could.

Part 7

"I come as one

I stand

as ten thousand."

Maya Angelou

38

1853

Kø had time to reflect on the incredible issues of his life once he was aboard *The Metrova*. The plan to stay for seven days had to be cut short to five whirlwind days in Copenhagen.

Harald and his brothers heaved a sigh of relief when they saw their father aboard *The Metrova*. General Sønne understood that no charges were to be pressed and as quickly as they were brought aboard the ship, the four men left and waited in the boat below as Hans and Kø said their final goodbyes. Foremost, Kø knew that he wasn't 'an accident of trade.' He was no 'inconvenient shadow.' He was his father's beloved son. Whether he was black, or white didn't matter anymore. The fact was, that he was both white and black in an equal measure. But above all, he was his own man. His life, his present and his future were in his hands, and he would make the best of it as he possibly could.

It still amazed him, that after just a week of knowing her, that Conrad was really serious about marrying Daffodil. Conrad's father was a Danish Jewish merchant who had also traded on the Guinea Coast. He had three children with his African wife and had sent all three to study in Denmark. Conrad, the first born, had just finished studying Law. After they married, he and Daffodil planned to build an inn which Daffodil would run, while Conrad would practice his trade.

"This is where we part, my brother," said Daffodil when she finished packing all her belongings. King Mingo's men loaded the large trunks into a large boat that Conrad Wulff had hired.

"You know you always have a home wherever I am," Kø whispered to her pressing a medium sized package into her hand. "Send a telegraph if you need me."

"What is this?" Daffodil asked.

"This is what I negotiated for from the General and my brothers. Half of it is yours."

Daffodil gasped, surprised.

"And Pa will be there for you. He has promised to give you away at your wedding. His fourth son may be leaving, but he has gained a daughter."

"Hey, Kø!" Conrad Wulff said good-naturedly, when their embrace lasted longer than expected.

"Can I have my fiancée now? I need to take her home with me!"

As *The Metrova* sailed toward Africa, everyone stood on the stern waving. Daffodil held Conrad's hand tightly as she waved. With tears streaming down her face, she continued to wave, even when the ship dipped beyond the horizon.

39

August 12ᵗʰ, 1853

It was just before dawn that the lookout on duty shouted the words that the people aboard *The Metrova* had waited a lifetime to hear.

"Land!!!"

The roar of joy and victory, which Kø and all those who left the Danish Virgin Islands let out when they saw the West African coast, shook *The Metrova* all the way down to the booty that lay in the hold. Every man, woman and child crowded on the deck to look out at their homeland. The golden sand looked soft, warm and inviting and coconut trees swayed gently in the wind. There was not a dry eye on *The Metrova* that day.

Fishermen, fishmongers, stragglers, hawkers, and their customers dotted the Quitta beach. They looked up curiously at the ship that had berthed a mile or so away. They thought it was another batch of explorers seeking their fortune and they quickly sent word to the King. They were puzzled when the first batch of strangers in the canoe was all black people, and they stopped to observe the newcomers.

Sitting on a mat, not too far away, a little boy played with a miniature ship. Something was vaguely familiar about the boy and the ship he played with, and Kø stopped mid-stride to take another look at the boy. He was brown-skinned and handsome, and his hair was soft and shoulder length already. He must have felt the eyes on him because the boy suddenly got up and toddled toward Kø, holding out the ship. The little boy smiled at the handsome stranger, and it was like a déjà vu. The boy's lopsided smile and the deep dimples were instantly familiar.

Just as recognition began to dawn, out of the corner of his eye, Kø registered a sudden movement – a woman with dark ebony skin began to run toward the boy. She reached him in record time, snatched up her son and held him close. Breathing hard, she looked at the strangers. Kø and Eva's eyes met. And it was as it was, when they first met, a meeting of souls.

"Køooooo!" she screamed.

"Evaaaaa!"

Eva and Kø stretched out their arms at the same time. Their son, still holding the miniature ship his father had made before he was born in hand, stretched it out toward his father. Kø engulfed both of them in a tight embrace. Their tears mingled with joy and laughter. Every lamentation became a celebration as their arms circled each other again and again in a tight embrace.

"Køndo gbor! Køndo has come back!" Eva wept.

"You came back!" she cried. "You came back to me!"

"Your Dada came back!" she said to her son.

"I gave you my word, didn't I, Eva?"

Boussy put his arms around Kø and his young family. Ezekiel embraced them and looked up to the heavens in profound gratitude. Then came a woman sitting on the beach. She folded her arms around them in welcome. Her friends joined her. King Mingo joined the embrace.

"Køndo went to the land of the white man. And he is back! He came back to us!"

The news reverberated around the town.

"Help me up!" Metrova told her maid.

"You are not going to walk to the beach, are you?"

"I will if you help me up!"

"You can hardly walk Ma'am, your son will come to you!"

"Fetch me my most beautiful white cloths… immediately!" Metrova insisted. "And fetch me my cane!"

And so they helped her up and she donned her whitest celebratory attire. Her footsteps were slow and painful. But she no longer felt pain. Her son came back. Slowly, she walked singing and dancing with an entourage of triumphant women, all the way to the beach, where they joined the ever-expanding embrace.

> *You've been long gone; it's an empty home,*
> *Come on back where you really belong.*
> *You are always welcome home,*
> *Welcome home.*

> *You've been kept down for much too long,*
> *Stand up please and say I am free.*
> *Don't forget you are welcome home,*
> *Welcome home!*[29]

Canoe after canoe emptied the newcomers in from the ship. Family, friends and curious observers poured onto the beach to witness the one-of-a-kind arrival. The spontaneous embrace of the natives and the newcomers grew and formed concentric

---

[29] Song 'Welcome Home' by Ghanaian band Osibisa. Composed in 1972 by Mac Tontoh, Teddy Osei and Sol Amarfio.

circles, till the newcomers and the inhabitants enmeshed into one.

Standing in the middle of the embrace was Kø, still holding tight to his family.

The warrior had finally come home!

Research Resources

1. Daughters of the Trade: Atlantic Slavers and Interracial Marriage on the Gold Coast by Pernille Ipsen

2. Closing the Books by Governor Edward Carstensen on Danish Guinea, 1842-50

3. The Ugly Duckling by Hans Christian Andersen

4. Caribbean Slavery in the Atlantic World. A Student Reader. By Verene Shepherd, Hilary McD. Beckles

5. Property Rights in Pleasure: The Marketing of Enslaved Women's Sexuality. By Hillary McD. Beckles

6. 'We be wise to many more tings'. Blacks' Hopes and Expectations of Emancipation. By Woodville K. Marshall

7. Slaves' Use of Their Free Time in the Danish Virgin Islands in the Later Eighteenth and Early Nineteenth Century. By N.A.T Hall

8. Black Women, Economic Roles and Cultural Traditions. By Sidney Mintz

9. Ships through the ages, by Lobley Douglas

10. Wikipedia

Made in the USA
Columbia, SC
18 June 2020